A Likely Story

Deborah Nock

MWA

Cover illustration by Natalie Davies,
Birmingham, West Midlands, UK

Cover layout by Nathan Pretlove,
Winter Hill Design, Telford, UK

Copyright © 2020 Deborah Nock
All rights reserved. No part of this book may be
reproduced or used in any manner without
written permission of the copyright owner,
except for use of quotations in a book review.

To Mom and Dad

With all my love, and
thanks for the bedtime stories

CONTENTS

The Truth Behind the Gold	1
A Tall Tale	15
Fool's Gold	33
The Wild One	53
Locked Away	75
A Pesky Problem	95
The Simple Truth	113

ACKNOWLEDGEMENTS

I can't believe it, my second book! I never thought I'd overcome my natural laziness long enough to write one, let alone two. As ever, encouragement from everyone in the Pub motivated me to write these true stories behind the fairy tales. So thank you Angela for creating such a wonderful place. Amanda and Xanthe are lovely ladies who read the first few stories and luckily liked them enough for me to carry on with the others. Kimberly and Jim read the finished article and provided valuable comments, thank you so much. David, you're a star for letting me name a character after you, it won't be forgotten I'm sure... Many grateful thanks to Natalie for such a wonderful cover image, it truly is amazing and the book wouldn't be the same without it. And to Nathan for making the cover design come together.

Finally, much love to John and Adam – you bring me happiness every day.

THE TRUTH BEHIND THE GOLD

'Hello? Hello, can you hear me? Is this thing working? Ok, ok, there's no need to roll your eyes, I was only checking. And tapping your fingers like that isn't going to relax me. I'm nervous, can you blame me? I've been hiding in the shadows for a very long time.'

'How did you track me down, anyway? Not that it really matters, you've found me now. And it's time the truth came out. No more dragging my name through the mud. I want people to know who I am, what really happened those many years ago. So, where to begin? My name, I guess. It's as good a place as any.'

'My name…is Rumpelstiltskin. Stop glaring at me, I know what you're thinking. A small, bandy-legged, imp-like creature who could turn straw into gold and tried to steal a baby? Yep, that's me! Well, that's the me that history remembers, at least. Not the real me, of course. No, Orla saw to that.'

'What was that, you can't hear me properly? Well, what do you expect? After all this time, my voice isn't as strong as it used to be. Turn the volume up at your end, use your brains. Listen closely.'

'I'm not actually from this world. I'm from Tamaris, a small planet in the next galaxy. I was given the name Rumpelstiltskin at birth, but even by my race's standards I was on the short side. So, I grew up with the nickname 'Stumpy Rumpy'. Oh, how I hated it. Especially when my so-called friends would shout, "Run, Stumpy's coming!", then race off as fast as they could. I was never able to catch them. I usually ended up tripping over my long beard, face first into the mud.'

'Yes, I know I was only a child – but on my world, even children grow beards from an early age. We normally wrap them around our waist. Of course boys *and* girls, it's only natural. Stop interrupting and let me continue.'

'I grew up lonely, and so very angry. It's no wonder my face is always miserable in the stories, that much is true. I honestly thought my life would improve when I changed my name. Lorcan is much better, don't you think? It means 'little fierce one', and that's what I am. Inside, at least. But the damage had been done. I didn't have any friends, I couldn't find a job, and I was desperate for money. In the end, I decided that if people couldn't be bothered to help me, I would take what I wanted instead. I only stole from people who could afford it, where's the harm in that?'

'Anyway, the trouble really started when I was on the run after stealing from some of the Drangheta clan. They were the local crime lords on my world, and it was their only transmogrifier – a very useful device that can make any object look and feel like gold. Particularly handy if you live on the shady side of life.'

'You see, on every planet I'd visited, I'd noticed a strange fondness for the yellow stuff. Even *your* eyes lit up when I mentioned it. I knew I could make a fortune with the device – it could even make straw seem like gold. But the clan weren't best pleased that I'd stolen their most treasured possession. I'd been flying through space for weeks trying to escape. I remember one particular battle when they'd tracked me down to an old base on a rocky moon. I managed to slice one across the leg, almost took it off at the knee. But now their lasers were aimed directly at my head, I had no way of escaping. I was about to hand over the device and beg for my life, when all of a sudden…'

'You know what, you'll get wrinkles if you keep frowning at me like that. I get the message, back to the story.'

'Where was I? Okay, well my little spaceship was finally running out of fuel and I was getting desperate. No fuel meant a certain, icy death, forever drifting through space. But as luck would have it, I became trapped in a wormhole that flung me onto what I now know is Earth.'

'In fact, I found out later that many of my race had landed on this small, wretched rock. They established themselves as 'dwarfs' who lived underground and mined for gold. I suspect a few of them had transmogrifiers as well. They'd managed to teach the locals our language, which quickly caught on – handy for me, as it turned out.'

'To cut a long story short, my ship crashed, a wing fell off and I had no immediate way of fixing it. If I ever wanted to make it home again, I knew I had to find a way to make money fast to repair the ship. A difficult enough task in those uncivilised times, impossible if you were poor. Luckily, the transmogrifier wasn't damaged – so I made my fortune turning objects into 'gold'. Life was actually pretty good for a long time. The thought of going back to my miserable old life never even crossed my mind. Until a certain miller's daughter came along.'

'Orla was certainly a beautiful, golden-haired girl with a smile that could melt the hardest of hearts. But oh, she was wicked inside. As cold as ice she was, with the same ability to burn whoever got in her way. The only person she cared about was herself, and she used all her outwardly charms to get what she wanted. To my everlasting misfortune, she saw me use the transmogrifier one day.'

'You see, I had become rather greedy back then. I was wallowing in riches and living a life of luxury – but still wanted more. Nothing seemed to satisfy me. I had grown complacent, believing that anybody could be deceived. I hadn't counted on someone like Orla. She caught me one day when I had been conning some poor sucker into believing he'd be rich. She hid and watched as I transformed an old wooden spoon into gold. Unlike most of the women in those days, she didn't immediately faint or cry out, "Dark magic, burn him!" No, our Orla was made of much sterner stuff.'

'Instead, her greedy little heart recognised an opportunity to blackmail me and use the transmogrifier for her own wicked purposes. She wasn't after gold, that was far too commonplace for her. She wanted power, and lots of it. She managed to discover that I was a fugitive from another world, and that I'd be in serious trouble if the Dranghesi ever found me.'

'Oh come on, I'm sure even *you* would have confessed all if she'd sat on you and threatened to put hot pins under your toenails or pluck out your eyes. I am not a brave Tamarian, ok? Can I carry on now?'

'Anyway, she schemed and plotted and came up with a plan to trick the King into marrying her. Becoming Queen would guarantee that she would be able to control people's lives. Especially if the King's health was to suddenly deteriorate…'

'Well, there was no health service in those days you see. No-one would check if he'd *really* died of natural causes. She knew she could get away with murder, especially if she fluttered those beautiful eyes and acted all helpless and vulnerable. In fact, she'd already sourced the poison.'

'You all know the next part of the story, how the King came to hear of a poor miller's daughter who could spin straw into gold. Of course, it was all her idea – her father was far too stupid to come up with a plan like that. He did, however, dote on his "little angel" and would do anything for her. So, she made him put on his best smock (with just a smudge or two of dirt for that authentic touch) and ordered him to see the king and make that outrageous claim.'

'She knew, you see, that the King was a proud and vain man who loved the good life. What she couldn't know was that he was also desperate. He'd already spent most of the kingdom's riches on the finest clothes, swords, horses and food, as well as splendid new palaces and numerous statues of him in his 'manliest' poses. He was in dire need of covering up his crimes before he was found out and his head was cut off. Those were hazardous times, you know. Not surprisingly, he jumped at the chance of meeting her.'

'Orla's face must have been a picture when the King first ushered her into a room filled with straw, along with the stark warning, "Spin gold or die". She hadn't the faintest idea what to do with the strange contraption in the middle of the room. It wasn't until I bravely managed to sneak into the palace (admittedly past sleeping, snorting, dribbling guards – the King could no longer afford good security) that she found out it was a spinning wheel. With a look of distaste and utter contempt, she imperiously ordered me to get to work.'

'I expect you can guess that I used the transmogrifier? Turning straw into gold seemed so easy when you read the fairy tale, but it was no mean feat I can tell you. I spent hour after hour transforming each and every strand. I couldn't do it all at once – oh no, the transmogrifier didn't work like that. I could only work on a few strands at a time, waiting for it to cool down between batches to prevent it setting fire to all that dry straw. I was exhausted by the time I'd finished. Unlike Orla, who slept like the dead all night. "I need my beauty sleep, you withered imp," she told me. "Something you clearly know nothing about."'

'After that first night, the King's face lit up with greed at the sight of all that gold. He could barely contain himself. He ordered Orla to do the same the next night, "On pain of death". My heart sank, but somehow I managed to get through the even higher piles of straw while Orla once again slept all night, snoring like a pig.'

'The King was ecstatic, of course, and demanded more. To be honest, I think he would have been quite happy to carry on like that every night forever. But this time Orla put her foot down and demanded that he marry her if she did as he asked. I could see that she was finding the constant death threats rather tedious. The King somewhat reluctantly agreed and, once I had completed my final arduous task, married her the next day. Not because he loved her, although he did like to admire her lovely face, but as insurance for the future when he'd spent all that wonderful gold.'

'All was well for almost a year. Orla flaunted her power at every opportunity, inviting all her old acquaintances to the palace (she had no real friends) so she could show off, ordering her servants around to satisfy her every whim. Yet although poets sang about her beauty, she wasn't well loved. How you behave really does reflect what kind of person you are, and Orla's black heart meant she would never be truly beautiful or adored. The real power she craved eluded her.'

'I, on the other hand, was beginning to think I might have a chance at a happier life. I often spied on her before skulking through the secret passageways to meet her. Did I mention that the King had insisted on a new gold bale every week as one of the conditions of marriage? Anyway, watching her I soon realised that money wasn't ever what I really wanted, or power. It was love and friendship, which I'd never had as a child. I'd even begun to give up my thieving, cheating ways and had started to turn my life around.'

'Until the fateful day when Orla had a daughter. It was what queens were expected to do after all, produce an heir, but she was *not* happy. All the focus turned towards the child, away from her, and her fragile ego couldn't stand it. She quickly began scheming of ways to get rid of the "smelly, whining brat". She did consider abandoning the baby in the woods, but it was too risky and she knew the King would turn his realm upside down to find her – he genuinely loved his little girl. So she came up with another devious plan, again involving yours truly (of course…).'

'She knew Lorcan wasn't my real name. I had stupidly told her so when she'd given me too much strong…wonderfully sweet and tempting…mead one night. Her cunning scheme was for me enter the throne room, dramatically sweep the beloved Princess into a sack, and threaten to cast a wicked spell if the King tried to stop me. She predicted that he would immediately begin to weep and wail ("the snivelling coward"), all the time carefully presenting his most handsome, distraught side to his devoted followers. She would play her part by fainting gently to the floor in distress.'

'At this point, I was to "sneer wickedly but show a touch of pity, you need to be believable" and grant them a reprieve if the Queen could tell me my real name within three full moons. She was certain nobody would ever have heard it before. I was an alien after all, and no parent in their right mind would call a human child Rumpelstiltskin.'

'All went to according to plan, and Orla sobbed convincingly enough alongside the King in front of the crowd. But I shuddered to see the joyful glee in her eyes at the thought of discarding her unwanted daughter. The fairy tale is pretty much true at this point. She scoured the kingdom for weeks, pretending to search for my name. She left the babe at home though, so she could be centre stage and wallow in the lavish care and attention she received from all those who tried to console her. Wherever she went, she was waited on hand and foot, safe in the knowledge that no-one would ever guess my true name.'

'On the next two full moons, she read from an endless, dreary list of names. I had to shake my head wildly at each one, with a mad grin on my face. My neck muscles have never recovered, I can tell you. Especially on cold mornings. Oh, let me tell you about the agony I suffer...'

'All right, okay, there's no need to be so hard-hearted. I'll gloss over my terrible aches and pains, shall I, will that make you happy?'

'Also true to the tale, but most unfortunately for Orla, someone *did* discover my birth name one warm and balmy night. I had developed a taste for that honeyed, heavenly mead she had introduced me to, and was dancing drunkenly around a roaring campfire.'

'"My name is Rumpelstiltskin," I cackled and giggled inanely as I capered around the fire.'

'"My name is Rumpelstiltskin," I shouted, staggering too close to the flames and almost setting my beard alight.'

'"My name is Rumpelstiltskin!" I roared loudly to a mainly uncaring world, before keeling over and finally passing out besides the crackling flames, snoring loudly.'

'Or so I was later told. To my misfortune, a passing farmer had seen and heard everything. He'd at least done me the kindness of dragging me from the fire before I started to smoulder. But had then run straight to the King, gleefully rubbing his hands all the way at the thought of getting a large reward for saving his beloved daughter.'

'You can imagine his disappointment when the guards, who he'd assumed were leading him to the treasure room to take his pick, instead took him outside and tipped him into the smelly, noxious moat – the King was not a generous man. Stop laughing, I'm sure he didn't find it very funny.'

'I knew something was wrong the instant I walked into the room on that final full moon. The King's face was beaming, but if looks could kill I would have been skewered on the spot by the fearsome expression on Orla's face. She was clearly furious, but trying to look relieved and happy to keep up appearances. The sour, cheated expression that twisted her lovely face was a true reflection of her inner self, I always thought.'

'I strolled in as usual and began taunting the gathered throng by gleefully shouting "That's not my name!" to every suggestion they made. I have to admit, I quite enjoyed the theatrics of it all, strutting round the room while everyone showed me some respect for once. But then the King triumphantly cried out the final, true name. My heart skipped a few beats and I turned white with shock, then red with horror. Mostly in the sure knowledge of what Orla was going to do to me once she got her hands on me. But also because I swore I heard a few people snigger, "Stumpy Rumpy". Even here, I couldn't escape that blasted name.'

'Of course I didn't get so angry that I stamped my way into the middle of the earth, don't be ridiculous. And clearly I didn't tear myself in two in rage. What nonsense, I'm surprised you would even ask such a silly question.'

'Anyway…to everyone's complete surprise, the King didn't order his guards to chop off my head. I'll never know why for sure – but he had been studying Orla's face rather carefully that night. Maybe he suspected something? I didn't care, to be honest, because instead he banished me from his kingdom, with instant death if I returned. You can surely imagine my relief at no longer having to steal an innocent child from her family! But just as importantly, I'd been ordered to go where Orla could never follow. I would finally be free of the vile woman. While everyone was celebrating, and she was trying to choke down her bitter disappointment, I quietly sneaked away.'

'There isn't much more to tell you after that, to be honest. You've heard my tale now – the real one. After talking to you, I'm not quite sure I'm the nice guy I thought I was. Even back then, I knew I had to change my ways if I was ever to find real happiness. But Orla deserved everything that happened to her.'

'Unlike the fairy tale, the Queen didn't live happily ever after. Far from it. She had no choice but to look after the baby and it didn't take long for her disappointment and anger to transform her into a cantankerous, miserable, ugly woman.'

A Likely Story

'And what I'd 'forgotten' to tell her was that the transmogrification process is only a temporary illusion. After about ten years, everything returns to its natural state. Can you imagine the King's wrath when his precious gold turned back into straw? He became a laughing-stock and blamed Orla entirely. I'm pretty sure he was sick and tired of her spiteful, whinging ways by then. He ordered his men to drag her from his kingdom – literally drag her, with her hands and feet tied together. Like I said, tough times. They left her in a forest to fend for herself. She managed to undo her bindings and find an old cottage that she lived in for the rest of her days, plotting and scheming – until the fateful day she met Hansel and Gretel, of course.'

'Her daughter, free from Orla's malign influence, grew up to be kind and loving and captured the hearts of all who met her. She became more and more powerful as time went on, eventually ruling the land with a benevolent hand for many glorious years after her ageing father drowned while trying to grasp the 'gold' of the sun in the palace lake. That's the trouble with you humans, you live such short lives and your minds deteriorate rather quickly.'

'As for me, well things didn't work out quite as I'd hoped. The Dranghesi turned up one day, just as I was using the transmogrifier one more time. In my defence, I was down to my last few pennies and in dire need of a boost, just one last trick to set me up for life. But they caught me mid act.'

'They were surprisingly lenient after I told them my story. Once they'd stopped laughing and wiped the tears from their eyes, they gave me my freedom. Being the sucker in such a wonderful tavern tale was punishment enough, apparently. They removed what was left of my spaceship, so I could never escape, and took their transmogrifier with them, sniggering and whispering "Stumpy" among themselves as they left.'

'I was doomed to spend the rest of my life on this small, miserable planet. Never again would I see the purple meadows of home or the iridescent lakes shimmering under the gentle light of the blue moon, or smell the wonderful aroma of home-baked bariska. Instead, I'm stuck here living out my life, waiting for the end. We Tamarians are a very…very long-lived race, so it has been a long time indeed.'

'I have spent many years wandering this earth, slaving away at endless, tedious jobs. I never mixed with those of my own kind though. I kept myself to myself, and now I am tired. I've had a mostly lonely life. I did have a wife once, another outcast Tamarian like myself. But I couldn't stand her constant nagging to "get a job, do some work round the house, get out of that chair, you lazy slob", so I sneaked off one day to give my ears a rest and never went back.'

'I do have a new job though, I'm happy to say. My time with Orla gave me a taste for performing, and I recently managed to land a role in a film. I'll be dwarf number three in that new blockbuster being released next week. You'll see my alias in the end credits, I'm sure. But you know my true name now, and I'm glad to finally share it. My name…is Rumpelstiltskin.'

A TALL TALE

'Hello, can I help you? You're looking for Mr Blunderbore? Well, you've come to the right house, I am he. Although we rarely get any visitors out here, it's not the easiest of places to reach. Please do come in, it's cold out there. Here, let me take your coat, such beautiful fabric.'

'Why did you say you were here? Wait, don't tell me yet. I'll just hang this up, we can't have the place looking untidy.'

'There, that's better. I can't abide a mess, I really can't. An uncluttered home reflects a clear mind, I always say. Come this way to the drawing room, it's much warmer in there.'

'Would you like some tea? I have a lovely Earl Grey you might like. Perfect with a little drop of honey from my bees. And what about one of these delicious little cakes? My wife makes them, you know, her own secret recipe. Please, have two, I insist.'

'So how can I help you? If you don't mind me saying, those bags under your eyes tell me you've come a long way. I have some ointment that could soothe them, if that would help? No? Okay, well you just sit there and rest for moment, and tell me why you're here. You've piqued my interest.'

'What do I do? Why, I'm a scientist of course, I thought you knew that? Oh, what a shame. I was hoping that was why you'd come to visit. I rarely get the chance to talk about the weird and wonderful quantum world to anybody who understands.'

'Maybe you would like to see my laboratory at least? I'm rather proud of it. Come on then, it's this way. Mind the step. Let me just unlock the door. Blasted key, I really must get the lock fixed after the break-in. Ah, there we go. What do you think?'

'You're right, it is a grand sight. The quantum world may be infinitesimally small, but the apparatus I need to measure it is huge. I had this place specially built to accommodate it, just look at the height of that ceiling. You could almost believe that a giant lives here. Not that giants really exist, of course, apart from in fairy tales. Although after the rather spectacular results of my recent experiment, I suppose anything is possible.'

'What do I mean? I'm not sure I should tell you, to be honest. You might start to question my state of mind – I know I did for a while. No, I think it would be better if I simply showed you around instead, come on.'

'You know, you really shouldn't frown like that, it does nothing for you. You'll be old before your time if you carry on like that. If you insist, I will tell you what happened. But don't say I didn't warn you! Sit yourself down on that stool and listen closely.'

'The first strange incident occurred when I was walking late at night, as I like to do when my mind is preoccupied by a particularly knotty equation. While I was so delightfully preoccupied, I stumbled into a group of what I can only describe as a rather unsavoury bunch of scruffy ruffians. I was glad I had my walking cane with me for protection.'

'And they were so short, that's what struck me on second glance. Short men with long beards wrapped around their waists. I almost towered above them, and I am no giant as you can see.'

'Don't smirk like that please, it is most unbecoming.'

'Despite their height, one of them pushed me quite roughly against the tree and brandished a dagger in my face. I still have the bruise to this day. I protested strongly, of course, and told him I was a poor scientist with no money to steal. At which point, the rest of his motley crew began whispering excitedly and rudely jabbing their fingers in my direction. They were talking for so long that the cold set into my bones and my terror began to wear off. I was becoming quite impatient, if truth be told. If I'm going to die, I'd rather it was over quickly, not drawn out so uncomfortably in the dead of night.'

'I was just at the point of deciding whether to grab the dagger and break free, while my assailant was distracted by the conversation behind him, when they suddenly stopped talking and stared at me ferociously. My terror came back immediately, I can tell you. I broke into a cold sweat all over, which really wasn't good for my lovely silk shirt.'

'One filthy rascal with a bandage around his leg limped over and beckoned for me to lean down. "Fix our ship or I'll tear bloody holes in that fine shirt of yours!" he bellowed into my ear, which he had grabbed most painfully.'

'Well, what *could* I do, apart from agree to his demands? Besides, I was rather curious by then, as there wasn't any water for a ship to sail on for miles around. So, under duress and at the sharp end of the dagger, I followed them through the woods to a large clearing.'

'You can imagine my surprise when I saw a spaceship sitting there! I'm sure my jaw almost hit the ground. Never in my wildest dreams did I think I'd see such a thing. A beautiful, sleek little ship made to cruise the stars. The limping man told me the Dranghesi had been taking off from Earth to return home, when suddenly a hole appeared in the air and sucked them right through. They were understandably extremely confused as to how such a thing was possible, and all sorts of dire consequences were promised if they ever found out who was responsible.'

'Anyway, to cut a *very* long story short, it was actually a simple matter to fix the ship. The components were surprisingly similar to my great machines. To tell you the truth, I was feeling somewhat guilty.'

'You see, my latest experiment had backfired the previous evening. I thought I had finally managed to create a stable quantum wormhole, after a couple of failed experiments years ago, but I couldn't find out where it had manifested. That was why I was out walking that night, to try and discover my mistake. These men were undoubtedly victims of my blunder.'

'But I didn't have the heart to tell them that due to the nature of my experiment, they had actually travelled through time rather than space. In fact, I neglected to tell them that I had anything to do with the whole messy situation. I do value my life, you understand, and that dagger really was very sharp.'

'Luckily, I had the equipment to recalibrate their engines. They were incredibly grateful that I was able to repair their ship. Their leader dropped to his knees and grabbed me around the legs. His face streaming with tears (further adding to my guilt), he told me that the Dranghesi would be forever in my debt. As part payment, he gave me this very interesting device. Here, take a look.'

'He called it a transmogrifier and told me it could make anything look like gold. Well I was naturally dubious, of course, but it seems he was right! A lovely piece of engineering, I must say. I was studying it, in fact, when I first heard somebody trying to break into the laboratory, late the following evening.'

'I always work with the door locked, you see, especially after dark. You never know who to trust these days, and this equipment is exceedingly valuable. Yet I only lock that door with a standard key because the rest of the house is like an electronic prison. Nobody can get in from the outside without me knowing about it.'

'My heart began racing when I realised that somebody had somehow managed to infiltrate my defences without setting off the alarms. And I almost jumped out of my skin when the door handle rattled. The thin scraping noise that followed prickled the hairs on the back of my neck. It took me a few long moments to realise that someone was trying to pick the lock. Although I was scared, I shouted for them to stop or I would call the police. I may not be the tallest man around, but I *do* have a very loud voice when needed.'

'Did I manage to scare him away? Well no, as a matter of fact. As I stood in the shadow of one of my great machines (no, I didn't cower, thank you very much), I saw a pale young face press up against the laboratory window, surrounded by a mass of dark, unruly hair. I can still see the look of amazement at the size and grandeur of my equipment, his eyes were wide with wonder. But then they narrowed, and I knew what *that* look meant. Pure greed at the potential loot lying around.'

A Likely Story

'When the face disappeared, I ran over to unlock the door. I had to find the young scoundrel quickly, but quietly. My wife was sleeping soundly upstairs and, much as I love her, she can be terrifying if she's woken unexpectedly.'

'I poked my head around the door and listened carefully. The corridor stretched out before me, the solitary light from the laboratory becoming lost in the inky blackness. All I could hear was the low humming of my machines. Creeping quietly out of the room and into the dark, my hands trailed the wall so I would know where I was. I passed several doors, all locked, until I reached the stairs. As I sneaked by, intending to check the kitchen first before daring to go up, I heard a creak on the squeaky step – one that I had long ago learned to avoid, so as not to wake my wife. Heart beating wildly, I silently tiptoed upwards.'

'My heart sank when I heard a resounding crash as the boy fell against the little table on which my wife likes to keep her favourite flowers. It sank even further when her beloved voice bellowed out from her room. "What is all that noise out there, who woke me? Blunderbore, is that you stomping around like a herd of elephants? Wait 'til I get my hands on you, waking me in the middle of the night like this. Come here, you inconsiderate wretch." I heard a scuffle, ran up the final steps and switched on the hall light, ready to help my sweetheart.'

'Such a sight greeted me! My lovely wife, who is a rather large lady I must admit, was dangling a youth by the scruff of his neck, his feet barely touching the ground. I watched as her anger grew fiercer when she realised we had an intruder, and she began to violently shake him. The look of horror on that poor boy's face made me intervene, against any thoughts of self-preservation. "Please let him go, my love," I implored. "We don't want to hurt this one as well, do we? Put him down and we can sort this out peacefully."'

'It took her a moment or two to come to her senses. Her face, which had turned a rather alarming shade of red, returned to its normal rosy hue. With one last shake, she dumped the lad on the ground and glowered at him. "Explain yourself, boy. Why are you sneaking around our house, are you a thief?" she demanded, brandishing her meaty fist in his face.'

'Wisely staying silent, the boy quickly scrambled to his feet. After one last look at that ferocious face, he suddenly darted past me and disappeared down the stairs. "Quick, after him you fool. We can't let him escape unpunished," shouted my wife, and away she ran, the walls shaking as she stomped down the stairs.'

'As I watched, somewhat dazed by my wife's fury, the boy glanced behind and realised that the large, angry woman was rapidly gaining on him. He put on a burst of speed and dashed into the kitchen. "Ha!" cried my wife. "We have you now, you can't escape from there." She slammed open the door and stormed inside, with yours truly lagging a few steps behind.'

'Warily, the boy stood on the far side of the room,

keeping the large table between him and probable pain. He licked his lips and frowned, knowing he would be caught as we circled the table from opposite sides. Then he saw an open bag lying on the table, a few coins spilling out. I had been experimenting with the transmogrifier, you see. My favourite chocolate coins, turned to gold. His eyes lit up and a fierce, avaricious grin flashed across his thin face as he snatched the bag and dived under the table.'

'Rather agilely for such a large lady, my wife dropped to the floor and lifted the heavy tablecloth, ready and very willing to grab him. "Oh my goodness!" she exclaimed. "Blunderbore, is this your doing? Did you do this?" Confused, I bent down to have a look.'

'There, almost glowing in its transcendent beauty, was a perfect timehole in the floor. I gazed at it transfixed, thrilled that my experiment really had worked after all. My mind began to drift as I imagined the honours and reverence that would be bestowed upon me. My delightful reverie was broken when Mrs Blunderbore, who knew me well, poked me in the ribs.'

'I looked at her with reproach, rubbing at what would turn out to be a spectacular bruise. "Now is not a time to daydream, Blunderbore," she admonished. "I want this thing shut down, and I want it done now. Do you hear me? I don't want any more strangers traipsing round our home. Sort it out, or you'll be sorry." With that dire warning ringing in my ears, she stalked out of the room and back to her much-needed beauty sleep.'

'I sat back and sighed happily, captivated by the sight of a possible link to the past and amazed that *I* could have created something so magnificent. I longed to enter the timehole and discover for myself what wonders lay beyond, but I wasn't sure how stable it was. It could collapse while I was on the wrong side, and my courage failed me. Instead, I knew I had to look more closely at my research to find out more. And, if I wanted a quiet life, I would need to find a way to open and close the hole at will. I returned to my laboratory and pored over my notes until the sun rose and I fell asleep with my head resting on the bench, still none the wiser.'

'Mrs Blunderbore wasn't happy later that morning when she roused me from my restless slumber. "Blunderbore, you incompetent fool," she barked. "That hole is still open. You will keep a watch on it until you work out how to shut it down. Anyone else who comes through will not escape unharmed." She cracked her knuckles and, with a final warning look, stormed off into the garden and began attacking the weeds that had the cheek to grow there.'

'Yawning, I got to my feet and began searching for the motion detector I had bought some time ago when the foxes decided to visit. My wife, who can be somewhat ruthless, had been adamant that poison was the only way to deal with them, so I decided to scare them away before they could eat the tainted food. I wanted to use the detector to alert me if anyone else ventured through the hole while I worked on my equations.'

'I was just setting up the video feed on my computer, when on my screen a head suddenly appeared through the glow of the timehole. I watched as the young lad slid through onto the kitchen floor. He peeked under the edge of the tablecloth, presumably watching for signs of my wife. He was a brave youth, risking her wrath once more. Or foolish and greedy, more like. When he saw that the room was empty, he began searching to find more loot. I sat back, uncertain what to do next.'

'As I watched, nervously chewing my nails, Mrs Blunderbore passed by the laboratory window, a bunch of carrots in her hand. My skin went cold when I realised she was on her way to wash them in the sink. I sprinted to the kitchen and flung open the door. Gasping for breath (I'm not as fit as I used to be, you know), I whispered hoarsely, "Quick, run. She'll be here any moment." The boy froze, his hands on the dish of golden eggs that lay in the cupboard – the results of another of my experiments with the transmogrifier. Then, with a cheeky smile and an impudent wink, he whisked the eggs into his bag and disappeared again under the table, moments before my wife barged in and began to vigorously scrub the carrots. "We will be having casserole for dinner, Blunderbore," she told me. "Fetch that chicken that's been hanging in the pantry so I can prepare it." She turned and looked at me, and gave me that radiant smile that I had fallen in love with. I trudged off to do her bidding, neglecting to mention our little visitor.'

'For the rest of the day, I worked on my research, flitting between pages of closely-written equations and twiddling the knobs on my great machines. The solution continued to elude me and I was becoming rather frustrated. It was with great relief that I heard my wife call me to the sumptuous dinner she had prepared. Afterwards, drowsy and replete, we curled up together on the great sofa in front of a roaring fire and fell soundly asleep.'

'I woke with a start some hours later, and groggily looked around. The fire had burned down to smouldering embers, and it was getting chilly. Wondering what had woken me, I slipped out from under the bulk of my gently snoring wife, careful not to wake her, and covered her with the blanket warming by the fire. I crept out of the room and into my laboratory, intending to carry on with my work. After locking the door behind me, I chose some classical music to play on my tablet and quickly lost myself in tachyons and quantum entanglement.'

'I'm afraid I screamed rather loudly at the jarring crash that echoed round the room when the lock splintered in the frame. I spun round to see the youth standing there, a crowbar in his hands and shock on his face to see me still awake. We both froze for a few moments, listening for any sounds of movement from my wife. When I realised she was still sleeping, I sighed and beckoned for him to come closer.'

'"I won't hurt you," I promised as he warily crept into the room. "But I can't say the same for Mrs Blunderbore. So let me shut this door to lessen any noise, and then you can tell me more about yourself. And why you keep stealing from me!" I added, looking at him sternly over the top of the glasses perched on the end of my nose.'

'When he realised that I was relatively harmless, he squared his shoulders and sauntered over to my desk, carelessly swinging the crowbar by his side. "What is this magical item?" he asked, picking up my tablet, which had been charging in the sun all day. "It plays such beautiful music." As he stood there, enthralled by the wondrous melody rolling around us, I asked him his name. "Jack Durden," he replied dreamily, half hypnotised. Then he looked at me properly, and proudly declared, "Remember that name, I'll be famous one day."'

'Being the polite gentleman I am, I introduced myself. "Jack, I am Mr Blunderbore. Can you tell me more about yourself? Jack! Listen to me," I demanded loudly, trying to get through his musical daze and desperate to know more about *when* the other end of my wormhole had appeared.'

'Startled as my voice finally penetrated, Jack lost his grip on the tablet and fumbled about trying to catch it, throwing his crowbar onto the table so he could get a better grasp of the precious music maker. I watched in horror as the heavy metal crashed into the rows of test tubes found in every laboratory, it seems. As the sound of the glass shattering and tinkling echoed around the large room, we stared at each other anxiously, waiting for the inevitable.'

'"Go, before she finds you here," I urged, beginning to

shoo him towards the door. "I won't be able to stop her this time." Jack looked at me, and then at the tablet still in his hands. Flashing me another of those mischievous grins, he grabbed his troublesome crowbar and sprinted to the hallway. I heard him gasp as he saw Mrs Blunderbore moving towards him, her large bulk almost seeming to reach the ceiling, she was so angry.'

"'Come here you wretched urchin, you'll be sorry you ever trespassed in MY house," she thundered. She came to an abrupt halt as her house coat caught on the door handle nearest to her.'

'Seeing his chance, Jack darted once more into the kitchen. Mrs Blunderbore roared in frustration and the heavy fabric of her gown tore as she angrily ripped it away. Moving surprisingly swiftly for such a large lady, she crashed open the kitchen door and threw herself at Jack as he scrambled under the table. I followed at a safe distance, ready to step in should she require assistance. With a cry of triumph, she grabbed hold of one dirt-streaked leg and began to pull him backwards. Frantically, he lashed out with the crowbar, desperate to escape her clutches.'

'I was horrified by the anguished shriek of pain from my darling wife, a sound that will never leave me, I'm afraid. I should have done more to help her, but I have always been a timid man and she is so much more capable than me. I rushed over to her aid, to see a long, deep gash in her forearm where the crowbar had sliced into her skin. The blood flowed and dripped onto Jack's leg, who still lay there, shocked by what he had done. His eyes were full of sorrow and remorse as I looked at him reproachfully.'

'"I'm so sorry," he whispered to Mrs Blunderbore, his breath hitching, before he crawled further into the wormhole and out of our lives forever.'

'I rather enjoyed taking control after that. Gathering my poor, pale wife into my arms, I staggered back to the living room and gently dropped her onto the sofa. After building up the fire, I washed and bandaged the wound then stroked her hair until she fell asleep, her fingers entwined in mine until slumber finally relaxed her grip. Rubbing my white fingers, trying to coax the blood to flow once more, I returned to the laboratory and worked on my equations all night.'

'Mrs Blunderbore was so proud of me the next day when I showed her that I'd managed to close the wormhole – or timehole, I suppose I should call it. I'm still trying to discover how to properly open and close them though. They aren't very stable, I'm afraid. I'm close to the solution, I just know it. A few more experiments should crack it.'

'You know, it strikes me that my story isn't exactly news to you. Why *did* you come to visit me on this cold and blustery day? Not just for the pleasure of my company, I am sure. Let us retire to the drawing room, as I would very much like to hear your reasons for being here.'

'Let me get this straight. After hearing my tale, you think my experiment may have formed the basis of Jack in the Beanstalk? That back in his own time, Jack lived off tall tales about the giant who almost ate him?'

'Well I never, what an incredible theory. I suppose it could be possible, what with the golden coins and eggs. And I can even see that my tablet might have been transformed into a magic harp over the years.'

'But do you honestly believe that Mrs Blunderbore is the giant in question? Well really, what a shocking thing to say. My darling wife is the sweetest, kindest soul I know, and probably wouldn't hurt a fly. I am quite offended that she might be regarded as a big hairy giant.'

'In fact, I can hear her approaching, can you? Yes, those wine glasses are tinkling rather loudly, aren't they? She must be getting closer. Maybe you should slip out of that side door over there? No, really – I insist. Hurry, before she finds you here. She isn't in the best of moods this morning. Let me just grab your coat. It really is a wonderful fabric, so soft and silky. Thank you for listening to my story, but I shall have to bid you goodbye. Quickly now!'

'Why hello, my dear. Who was I talking to? Oh, just myself as usual. You know what I'm like. Now, how about a nice cup of tea and some of your delicious cake while you tell me about your day?'

'Whose cup is that? Well...mine, of course. I was rather

thirsty so I had two cups. Now don't glare at me like that, my love, you know it unsettles me. And cracking your knuckles will *not* do your arthritis any good. I can see you're in no mood to talk, so I'll be in my laboratory should you need me. Yes, I will be locking the door, I think that would be wise, don't you, dear?'

FOOL'S GOLD

'Out the way before I drop this load on your foot. Blimey, can't a man do some honest work in peace for a change? You'll get hurt if you keep hanging around here. Go on, shift it.'

'Look lady, I ain't got time to mess about. I don't want to talk to you, all right? And you'd better scarper before the foreman sees you. I will *not* be happy if he docks my wages for dawdling, you understand?'

'You're bloody stubborn, you know that? If I agree to meet you later, will you leave me in peace? The tavern down that alley in an hour, okay? Yes, it is a bit dark but I'm sure a big girl like you can cope. Just tell 'em Wolfie Wadsworth sent you, they'll leave you alone.'

'I saw that smirk. I'm big, I'm hairy, they call me Wolfie. No imagination round here, love. Now go!'

'Here's your drink, careful now. Yeah, it don't look good but it could taste worse. Best to knock it back quickly, I've found. Go on, fill yer boots.'

'Wow, sorry. Didn't expect you to react quite like that. Here, take this rag and wipe those tears, don't mind the dirt. No, I'm not laughing, honestly. Yes, it is a bit strong, isn't it?'

'Come on then…what's got you so agitated that you need to talk to someone like *me*? I'm a nobody, and not much use to anyone these days. Not since…'

'You know what? It don't matter. It's in the past and I'm steering clear of her now. 'Ere, you're not one of them reporter types, are you? 'Cos you'll be sorry if you are. Ruined my life with that story, they did. Can't trust 'em to tell the truth, they only write what sells papers. And me being the ugly one meant I made a great villain. The public lapped it up, of course.'

'Oh…well, thanks I guess. Glad you don't think I'm too hideous. But the whole affair still makes me mad, and I'm stuck in this dump taking orders from that snivelling bully of a foreman because of it. You should see him, tugging his forelock when the Governor visits the dock, pathetic. But I still have to ask, "how high" when he tells me to jump, or I don't eat. Anyway…what do you want?'

'The truth about Red? I knew it! You *are* one of those lowlife, good-for-nothings. I'll tell you what, lady. I won't lose my temper and we'll part ways right now. You really don't want to see an angry Wolfie.'

'Get yer hand off my arm before I rip it off. This lot wouldn't bat an eyelid if I was to chuck you in the docks.'

'What did you say? That's impossible. Nobody knows about those golden eggs but me and Red. And I know she'd never tell the story, her ego couldn't take the blow. Just who *are* you, exactly?'

'Okay, okay, I'll tell you. No need to look at me like that. Blasted women…bane of my life. Have another sip of that brew, if you can stand to, and I'll tell you everything.'

'I'm bad, always have been. Could never seem to hold down a job without losing my temper with the idiots around me. So I led a life of petty crime. A bit of burglary here, the occasional mugging there. I tried not to damage anyone too much. I just needed money, a man has to eat.'

'My family were rich once, you know. Owned a manor and everything. But there was a scandal, or so I was told, and the Lady disappeared, never to be seen again. The butler went on the run with the Lady's son, and his…my family have been running ever since. We've certainly never been on the right side of the law at least, put it that way.'

'My real troubles, though, didn't start until I met Red. It was only a nickname, but it suited her. I remember the first time I saw her, sitting on the dock with the setting sun lighting up that fiery red hair of hers. I was smitten the moment I laid eyes on her. She saw me staring like a lovestruck loon, and gave me a secretive smile that sealed the deal.'

'Which, of course, had been her plan all along. She needed a body to do the hard work during her various heists, and I was simply the latest fool who would have done anything for her. Well, not *quite* anything, as you'll find out.'

'We spent several happy months together, plundering the city and living the good life on our ill-gotten gains. But as much as my heart yearned, I only ever got a kiss or two from my beloved Red. The promise of more kept me dangling. I was content enough, even so. Until her greed for the fabled golden eggs destroyed my life.'

'I was poring over our plans for the next job when she claimed they weren't just a tall tale. She always came up with the grand ideas, and I would work out the details so we wouldn't get caught. I loved my work, I have to say. Gave my brain a good workout. I may be big, but I'm not stupid.'

'Yeah, yeah, I know. Love made me witless for a while. But just that once, mind. Never again.'

'She'd been talking to some bloke in the tavern, who told her the eggs were real. No doubt his tongue had been loosened with an ale or two and a few sweet sighs in his ear. She was good at that kind of thing.'

'He'd been working for one of the crime bosses, known as Young Jack 'The Bard' Durden because of his wild stories about magic holes, giants and golden eggs. Everybody laughed at him…quietly and behind closed doors. Jack was the kind of man who nobody crossed if they wanted to live with all body parts intact. You know the type – cocky, clever, and seemingly heartless.'

'No-one knew how he'd made his fortune, and few dared to pry. But some had heard whispers that the stash of golden eggs *was* real. Including our man, whose self-preservation had been whittled away by the curvaceous Red. Just the promise of a night spent with her made his lips flap, and he drunkenly told her where the eggs might be hidden.'

'He was probably rather surprised when her knife slid between his ribs as he was walking her home. When she begged me to dispose of the body, I didn't have the will refuse, no matter how unsavoury the task. Especially when she wriggled into my arms and looked at me so beseechingly.'

'Then she casually mentioned the eggs, and told me we were going to steal 'em.'

'While I was weighing down the body with large rocks stuffed into his ragged clothes, I wondered if I could scare her out of the crazy idea. I knew Jack's reputation, he would tear us apart if we tried to rob him. If he found out, of course. We were good, me and Red, but I wasn't sure we were that good. Not that it made any difference, she would never willingly abandon such a juicy prize.'

'As I absentmindedly pushed the heavy body into the oily water, which sank with a faint gurgle, my mind worked over the possibilities. Like I said, I enjoyed a puzzle and the added danger admittedly gave it a bit of spice.'

'By the time I'd walked back to Red, a plan had begun to form.'

'The first phase went without a hitch, and we managed to sneak into his mansion without being caught. But disaster struck when Jack, who was supposed to be out for the evening, returned home in a fine temper, storming into his study, flinging his wig onto the floor in a cloud of powder, and demanding his manservant bring him wine.'

'A few feet above on the gallery, Red huddled closer to me, her breath soft on my wrist while I carefully peered through the balustrade. The board beneath me creaked and I froze, not daring to shift my weight any further.'

'The finely-carved post I was gripping dug into my sweaty palms as Jack frowned and began to turn his head. Luckily, he was distracted by his man putting a crystal decanter of rich, red wine onto the table next to him. After instructing that he wasn't to be disturbed under any circumstances, he relaxed into the large, comfortable chair and closed his eyes.'

'My thighs were just beginning to cramp when he sprang back up and bolted the study door. Striding over to the vast bookshelf, he pulled on certain books in sequence. We weren't at all surprised when a secret door swung open.'

'Our newly-deceased informant had already revealed that this was where Jack kept his most precious possessions. Including the golden eggs, which he'd seen after slipping into the study one evening to nose around, while Jack was out on business. He'd frozen in terror to find his boss sitting there, the eggs gleaming in his lap as he lovingly polished them, the secret door wide open. When Jack noticed him, he went wild. Shouting for his guards, he stashed the eggs back in their hiding place before two burly men raced into the room. The beating that followed could not have been pleasant, but he was lucky to escape with his life. He'd been drowning his sorrows in the seedy tavern when Red found him. Unfortunately for him, as it turned out...'

'Below us, Jack stalked into the small space, muttering quietly, and returned with a small, rectangular device cradled protectively in his arms. Almost reverently, he placed it on the table, sat in the comfortable chair next to it, then gently swiped his finger across the strange, smooth surface.'

'The sweet, unearthly voice that resonated around us startled me badly. My hair bristled as the notes soared around us, filling every corner of the room. I could feel Red shift uneasily beside me. Despite the heavenly sound, I knew Jack must have made a pact with the devil – it weren't natural, that thing. Stretching out his legs, he leaned back and sighed contentedly. His look of bliss quickly turned to fury when he saw my white face staring between the posts.'

'Knowing I had no choice, I threw myself over the balcony and crashed onto the chair, knocking the wind out of the much smaller man. I winced as my elbow cracked onto the device, the music abruptly ending. While he was struggling for breath, I knocked him out with one clean blow, then tied him up while Red swiftly climbed down the wooden ladder. For added security, I gagged and blindfolded him. If he ever discovered who we were, we were dead.'

'"Quick," she hissed, pointing to the dark chamber. "The eggs will be in there, I'm sure of it. Go and get them while I keep watch for that manservant." I gave the restraints one last tug, then slipped into the small room.'

'Five golden eggs shone in the warm glow seeping from the study. I stared at them open-mouthed, knowing just one would bring us untold riches. We had to get out of there, fast. Heart racing, I snatched them up and raced back into the light.'

'To my horror, Red was standing behind Jack, a fistful of hair pulling back his head and a wickedly sharp knife at his throat. I watched in dismay as a small drop of blood glistened on the edge of the blade. "No!" I growled, leaping over to grab her arm, dropping the eggs on the way. "You can't stab a man while he's tied up, that's stone-cold murder."'

'Red sneered, and tried to break free of my grasp. "You fool," she spat, writhing furiously. "We can't leave him alive, he'll find us and kill us." In disgust, I wrestled the knife away and flung it into the hot embers smouldering in the fireplace.'

'I think it was then that the fog of love truly began to lift. Red's face twisted in contempt as she looked up at me, the ugly snarl distorting that lovely face. I shuddered and quickly dropped her arm. "Pick up those eggs," she ordered, rubbing the bruised skin. "We need to get to Granny's while we still can." Heart hurting, I bent down to gather them up.'

'As I stowed them safely in my pocket, I realised I could only find four eggs. Looking around, I noticed broken eggshell by the chair leg, fresh yolk spilling over the wooden foot. I sat back on my heels and stared in confusion, wondering where on earth it could have come from. I turned to Red to show her, but a commotion outside distracted me.'

'A fist banged on the door and a deep, gruff voice asked whether the Boss was okay. I looked at Red, eyes widening, then went to shift a heavy cupboard in front of the door, the broken egg slipping from my mind. As I strained to move its bulk, Red dashed over to the window and opened it wide, smearing blood on the plush curtains. Putting her fingers to her lips, she ran to the large fireplace and pointed frantically upwards.'

'My heart sank, knowing that the window was a diversion and that she wanted to climb up to the roof instead. I'd spent some time as a sweep when I was young, and knew how tight those spaces could get. Sighing, I boosted her up, then dragged myself after her into the darkness.'

'I only got stuck once, my shoulders wedged in a slight bend, soot raining down on my face. After a few desperate moments of painful squirming, I managed to slip free, Red tugging at my one free arm, her nails gouging deep into my skin. Part revenge, I think, for thwarting her plan to do away with Jack. If she'd had her way, I'd be stuck there still. But I had the eggs in my pocket and there was no way she was leaving *them* behind.'

'Panting, I hauled myself up the last few feet and flopped out onto the roof. Red stood there glaring, hands on hips as I tried to recover. "Get up, you brute," she urged, kicking me with her foot. "And don't drop those eggs, or your life won't be worth living." Wearily, I climbed to my feet and followed her carefully over the slippery tiles.'

'It was hard, treacherous going in the dark. I only just caught her hand when she misjudged her step and fell over the edge, arms flailing. As I stared down at her pale face framed in that wondrous hair, a small part of me was admittedly tempted to let her drop. I could be away with the eggs, free to live my own life, maybe find somebody who truly appreciated me. But her wide, frightened eyes were my undoing and I pulled her back onto the roof. I often wish I'd chosen a different path that night.'

'Hearing loud voices below us, I knew we didn't have much more time. As luck would have it, the branches of a large tree lay just within reach of the roof, and we scrambled across and shimmied down the wide trunk. With a last check to make sure the eggs were safe, we raced off down the dark alley and lost ourselves in the depths of the city, tensions between us running high.'

'Granny's place was an old, dilapidated wreck of a house from the outside, and wasn't much better inside. Until you reached the attic, that is. Every nook and cranny of that vast space was covered in opulence, most of it stolen, numerous lamps giving the warm room a welcoming glow. A door at either end led into the attics of the adjoining houses, escape routes should Granny ever need them, along with the hatch in the roof.'

'We never called her Granny to her face, of course. She would have slit the nose of anyone who tried. Her name was Aggie, and she was an old fence, one of the best there was at trading stolen goods for cold, hard cash. Red knew she could trust her to get a fair price for the eggs. For a large cut, no doubt.'

'When we knocked on her door that night, using the secret knock known only to wrongdoers like us, we heard a muttered groan, then the thump of a wooden leg across the floorboards. It took her some time to unlock the many bolts on the door.'

'When it finally opened an inch, her sweet, old lady face peered through the crack, one last thick chain holding the door in place. "What do you want, my dears?" she asked, her voice frail and feathery. "How can old Aggie possibly help anyone at this time of night?"'

'Red sighed and rolled her eyes. "Knock it off Aggie, it's us. We need your help, and quickly." Seeing her reluctance, she added, "There'll be a big bonus in it for you." As ever, that did the trick and she unchained the door to let us in, eyes darting everywhere to make sure we hadn't been followed.'

'"Right," said Aggie bluntly, slamming the door and straightening up, all business now. "What have you got for me this time?" She stood there impatiently, while I fumbled the eggs onto a soft cushion lying on the wide bed. A low whistle escaped her lips as the gold caught the soft light of a lamp and shone like fire. "Oh my," she whispered. "I thought those were merely another yarn from that young fool. Seems he wasn't fibbing after all." The wooden leg made bending awkward as she sat to pick one up. As she reached out, Red grabbed her arm and brought her face close to Aggie's.'

'"No tricks, I know you," she warned, her voice low and threatening. "There are four eggs, you will take one for your services. I want full market value for the rest, get me? Anything less and I will kill you." With that stark warning, she dropped the arm and strode over to the fireplace.'

'Aggie looked at me and raised an eyebrow. Then she turned to the eggs and picked one up to feel its weight and gauge its worth. "It's going to take me a little while to find a buyer for these, my dear," she drawled, smiling a little to see Red's back stiffen in annoyance. "Meet me at the coffeehouse late tomorrow afternoon and I will have the money for you."'

'She stood, cricked her back, then stumped over to Red. "One more thing," she said, gently turning the younger girl to face her. "If you ever threaten me again, I will slit your throat without a second thought."'

'Red licked her suddenly dry lips as the slim blade that

had appeared at her throat pressed into the tender flesh. "I'm…sorry," she breathed, and Aggie pulled back satisfied, after first drawing a small bead of blood. As she turned, she missed the dangerous look of fury that flashed over Red's face. I knew then there would be trouble ahead.'

'Aggie walked back to the pile of eggs and gently put them into a fleece-lined basket. "I can finally retire," she murmured wistfully. "Get out of this dump and back to where I truly belong." She looked at us both, then pointed towards the door. "Go on, clear off. An old woman needs her sleep."'

'As we were about to leave, Red turned back with a final threat. "I *will* be watching you, Aggie. If you disappear with those eggs, I'll hunt you down. You'll spend your retirement watching over your shoulder, waiting for my blade to gut you." With that, she whirled out of the door and disappeared down the rickety stairs. I followed with a heavy heart, yearning for a simpler life.'

'We spent much of the following day lying low, only venturing out to find food. The dark underbelly of the city was on high alert for those eggs, and word was that Jack was incandescent with fury.'

'Strangely, it was the loss of his devilish music maker that had him most enraged. He wanted the head of the brute that had killed it. Namely me. I begged Red to at least cut my hair so that I would be less shaggy and recognisable, but her thoughts were elsewhere and she barely acknowledged my request.'

'Time dragged as I watched Red pace up and down, muttering that she'd kill Granny if she double-crossed us. Finally I could take no more, and roared at her to stop. She halted mid-stride, shocked at the raised voice. I may be a brute, but I'm a softly-spoken one when not vexed. She glared at me, then stormed off. Sighing, I lay back on the bed to wait.'

'Red slipped her arm into mine as we strolled past yet another of Jack's men. They were out in force, looking for anybody suspicious, so we had decided to hide in plain sight. The coffee house was right next to the bank, and we knew that Granny would need to place our money in a safe deposit box. Not even *she* would dare to walk around carrying so much money.'

'So we'd dressed in our finery and Red had tamed my hair and beard with pomade. She was stunning in her green linen and silk dress, her face made even paler with white powder, the delicate cheekbones highlighted with rouge. Her wondrous hair was hidden beneath a tall white wig, precariously balanced it always seemed to me. In short, we were unrecognisable.'

'We meandered along, window shopping as we walked so as not to raise suspicion. Our only hiccup was a young boy who tried to lift Red's purse, containing nothing but her small, sharp dagger. Her nails dug into tender flesh as she tightened her grip on his wrist. "Get lost, little rat," she snarled, giving him a shake and flinging him away. Scrambling quickly to his feet, he gave her a reproachful look and disappeared into a dark alley.'

'When we eventually arrived at the coffeehouse, we asked for the private booth of Ms Brook, the name by which Aggie was better known in the exclusive establishment. Unlike most women, Aggie had somehow managed to gain the respect of the proprietors and was allowed to carry out her business freely. I am certain she was blackmailing them, she knew that information was more valuable than gold.'

'A smart young lad led us to the partly-enclosed table and asked if we would like some coffee. Never one to pass up anything free, I agreed. Red shook her head and ushered him away. We sat and waited for Aggie.'

'Before long, we saw her sweep into the room, a large basket hung over one arm. I looked at Red open-mouthed. Surely Granny wasn't bringing the money here. Or, even worse, the eggs themselves. Mouth dry, I furtively looked around to check we weren't being watched. As she approached, I saw the look on her face and my heart sank.'

'She was livid, high spots of colour on her cheeks that had nothing to do with makeup. Her steely blue eyes narrowed as they spotted us and she hobbled over, dropping the basket carelessly on the table. Taking a deep breath, she sat and carefully arranged her skirts. I watched fascinated as her jaws clenched, before she spat out, "What is the meaning of this trickery? How dare you try to deceive *me*." She whipped away the cloth to reveal four, plain brown eggs lying on the cushion.'

'We stared at her in confusion, then at each other. "Where are our golden eggs?" asked Red, her voice dangerously low. "Right there, you miserable wretch," replied Aggie, lips curling in contempt. "I don't know how you managed it, but somehow during the night, those 'golden' eggs of yours turned into these." She snatched one up and smashed it against the edge of the table. The fragile shell cracked, and yellow yolk oozed out over her wrinkled hands.'

'Unimpressed, Red tapped her long fingers on the table. "I'll ask you one more time…where are our eggs?" she demanded, then leaned forwards, tongue peeking out from between those luscious lips as she glared at the old woman.'

'Aggie grit her teeth and slammed her fist on the table, making us both jump. A couple of nearby businessmen looked up, but swiftly returned to their discussions. "These *are* your eggs," she growled. "I put them into my safe after you left, then went to sleep. When I awoke, these are what I found. Nobody could have tampered with them during that time, so you must have performed some witchery to try and fool me." She scowled ferociously at us both.'

'Red stared back, then quietly said, "That's impossible. They were solid gold, you held them." But then I remembered the strange broken egg I'd found in Jack's study and began to wonder.'

"Err, Red. She might be right," I stuttered, then winced as she angrily kicked my ankle under the table. "Don't give me that, Wolfie" she hissed furiously. "She's clearly trying to double-cross us. Do you really want to spend the rest of your life as a petty burglar? You're supposed to be the tough man – kill her if she doesn't tell her what she's done with those eggs.""

'I looked at her horrified. "No," I whispered back. "I'm a thief, not a killer. Besides, I'd be a fool to kill someone in broad daylight in a coffeeshop." I sat back and folded my arms, trying to gauge whether Aggie was telling the truth.'

'Rage washed over Red's face at my refusal to do her bidding, and the tension that had been building all day finally spilled over. Before I could stop her, she stood and slipped next to Aggie on the plush bench. Then, with a strangled cry, she plunged her knife deep into Aggie's side, twisting viciously from side to side.'

'As the blood flowed, and Aggie slumped lifeless on the bench, I sat in frozen in shock. To my eternal undoing because Red, realising her actions would have immediate consequences, leaped to her feet and cried bloody murder. When she saw men rushing towards her aid, she swooned convincingly at their feet.'

'From the outset, I was doomed. I was big, strong and *clearly* a killer. Unlike the trembling, harmless creature who accused me of stabbing old Aggie in cold blood. I was caught red-handed.'

'Except that I wasn't, of course. As one sharp-eyed Runner said to the judge, I didn't have a spot of blood on me when I was arrested not long after, so how on earth did I manage to kill Aggie so cleanly and efficiently? Nobody really suspected Red, of course, that sweet young woman. She had blood all over her, but insisted that was from when she went to try and help the gentle old lady. Apparently, I had lost my temper and savagely killed her when she broke one the eggs she had been so kind enough to give us from her own hens. My depravity knew no bounds, it seemed.'

'The papers in particular almost condemned me to the gallows. The public devoured the tales of a sweet old granny slaughtered by the wolf, while a naïve young woman watched in horror. Red relished telling stories of my supposed wickedness and debauchery. Even *I* would have assumed that I was guilty, especially after looking at the illustrations they drew of us both. My dark, brooding and convincingly menacing face contrasted well against Red's ravishing beauty and apparent innocence.'

'Everyone believed I was the villain…but there was enough doubt in the judge's mind that he couldn't convict me. Incredibly, he set me free – albeit under lifelong supervision.'

'That was ten years ago now, and I've spent the time trying

to forget while I've slogged my guts out at these docks. I never heard from Red again, of course, although I always hear *about* her. She runs a gang on the other side of the city now, thinks she's one of the big bosses. I know she stays out of Jack's patch though, she's not daft. I steer well clear of her myself, keep my head down. I don't want no more trouble.'

'I often catch myself wondering how those real eggs ended up in Aggie's safe though. I could have sworn they were solid gold when we left them, not painted or anything. I doubt old Aggie had anything to do with it, she knew that cheating your customers was a risky business. I'm still half convinced Jack made some sort of pact with the devil, that the eggs transformed back when we stole them from his possession. I know one thing for sure – they ruined my life, along with that treacherous Red.'

'So there you go, that's my story. Not that I expect you to believe me, nobody ever does. I will always be the villain to most people. How *did* you find out about me anyway?'

'Mr B sent you? Can't say I've heard that name before, which crew is he with?'

'Oh, I see…it's complicated, is it? I bet you've got a tale or two yourself, you have a look in your eye that I recognise. Troubled, that's what you are. Don't deny it, you wouldn't be in a place like this if you weren't desperate. Come on, you can tell old Wolfie.'

'Oh well, can't blame a man for trying. Hope you got what you wanted from me love, 'cos I've gotta go. That's the foreman over there, the one with the big, sweaty face. Seems I've spent longer talking to you than I realised. Maybe you could distract him with your feminine wiles, while I sneak out the back?'

'Ow, there was no need to slap, I was only kidding. Blimey, he's getting closer. Thanks for listening…but don't get telling anyone else, right? My reputation is damaged enough, without crazy stories of golden eggs and magic music makers.'

'Would yer mind moving your skirts so I can crawl past? Thanks lass, you're a good 'un. Stay safe getting out of here, there's some 'bad eggs' round these parts.'

'Oi, don't kick, it weren't that bad a joke. Listen girl, if you ever need help, you know where to find me. You and me would make a good team. If my boss don't kill me first. Farewell…and at least pretend you ain't seen me when he asks.'

THE WILD ONE

'What can I get you, my lovely? Tea and toast, is that all? Ok, coming right up! What's that you say, you want a quick word with me? I'm sorry my dear, I can't help you now. We're rushed off our feet, it's lunchtime. Do you want some jam with your toast?'

'Goodness me, you've been sitting there a long time. Would you like a top up, I've got a fresh pot here? There you go, that'll keep you going. What, you still want to talk to me? I can't imagine why. We haven't met before, have we?'

'Judging by *that* look, you're going to be very insistent. I tell you what, I'm due for lunch. If you can be patient for a moment, I'll go and ask my boss if we can sit somewhere quiet and have a little chat.'

'Right, come on then, over here. Sit yourself down. Oh, that's better, my feet were killing me. I'm getting too old for waitressing. Now, what on earth do you want to talk to me about…?'

'You've read my psychiatric reports? How dare you, that's private information. I shall sue my doctor for sharing it with you.'

'What? You hacked into the hospital computer? Why, that's even worse. I am going to call the police immediately.'

'Don't tell *me* not to get my knickers in a twist. How would you feel after such an invasion of privacy? Get out of my way, young lady. Now!'

'What do you mean, Alice was right? I don't normally shout and give orders, I'll have you know. I never once raised my voice to that blasted girl. So many lies have been spread about me because of her. Oh, for heaven's sake. Even after all this time, just the thought of her makes me lose my temper.'

'Why, of course I am still certain that my story led to *Alice in Wonderland* – despite the doctors telling me I was insane. There are simply too many similarities. I expect the author somehow heard a fantastical version of the truth, after Alice managed to escape justice.'

'You believe me? Why would you, when that was the reason the doctors locked me up for so many years?'

'Life has been a bit strange recently, has it? I can see in your eyes that you've been through a lot. Well, I suppose you may as well hear my story, it doesn't really matter now. I lost everything because of that girl, including my beautiful child,

A Likely Story

and I no longer care. Here's what really happened – the true story, not a fairy tale.'

'As you may or may not know, my name is Lady Mary Jenefer. I wasn't a queen, let me be clear about that. Certainly not a Queen of Hearts. I was simply a mother and the lady of the manor, responsible for the wellbeing of my villagers.'

'I like to think I was generous to them, always making time to listen to their problems. Not that I expect you to believe me after Alice's shenanigans. She was a wild spirit, that one. I still shudder remembering those wickedly green eyes peeking out from that shining halo of hair. Let me tell you how she arrived in our village.'

'We got most of this information from Alice during her trial, you understand. Yes, her trial – *not* the Knave of Hearts. Or my butler Wadsworth, as I prefer to call him. She had us completely flummoxed from the moment she arrived. We did anything she told us. Only Wadsworth's quick thinking saved us all. He was always clever, that dear soul. He managed to steal her mind control device, releasing us from her terrible influence.'

'Alice was a young woman from the future, you see. Many centuries ahead of us, from what I could gather. She did indeed fall through a hole, that much is true. A hole that was responsible for me being stuck here, I might add. But more about that later.'

'She had somehow managed to slip away from her

guardians, along with the 'treasure' she had stolen from them. While she was merrily wandering along the riverbank, singing and dancing to herself, a bright, shimmering hole appeared in the air. Her insatiable curiosity, of course, meant she couldn't resist stepping through it to see what happened. I'm sure the thought of danger never once entered her head.'

'I *do* think she was rather surprised to find herself in my turnip field though, the thick mud oozing between the toes of her bare feet and staining the hem of her simple white shift. But it didn't faze her, nothing did. Instead, she looked around for an opportunity to cause some mischief. Her sole reason for living, it seemed to me.'

'Her first unfortunate victim was old Jim, who was carefully weeding my plot like he did every day, bless him. Sammy, his little grandson, was at the top of the tallest apple tree, stuffing his belly. He saw the whole sorry episode. Alice apparently took a long look at a device dangling loosely in her hand, bit her lip, and glanced again at the ancient bent figure. Then she smiled that Cheshire cat grin of hers. I certainly know where the author got *that* idea from. She pointed the gadget at poor Jim, pressed the trigger and shouted, "You're a rabbit and…you're late, hurry up!"'

'Well, Jim apparently leapt up in shock (I can only imagine the cracking of his old bones), looked frantically at his non-existent watch and scurried away, muttering to himself that he would be "Too late, too late, oh dear". Alice fell about laughing hysterically, especially when Jim gave a few arthritic bunny hops along the way.'

'I guess people in the future have a different idea about entertainment. In my day, laughing at the misfortune of others was never acceptable. But then, Alice was always *quite* different, so maybe I'm being unfair. She was a clever girl, I'll give her that. And in her defence, she *had* been the main test subject in her institute. So it's no real surprise she was rather…unbalanced. We never did discover how she managed to get hold of the device. But we all suffered directly from the harm she caused using it.'

'Her success with Jim made her determined to see who else she could play with. She chased after him, leaving the glowing hole behind her without a second look.'

'When she eventually reached the village (after losing herself in the apple orchard), Jim was surrounded by his family and friends, all frantically trying to get him to stop him hopping and sit down before his heart gave out. At first, they had quite understandably thought the old man had lost his mind. Until little Sammy had come running up, panting out his story. On learning the truth, their immediate reaction was "Witchcraft!", and were trying every remedy they knew to counter the dark magic when Alice sauntered up.'

'Her grin grew even wider at the sight of poor Jim hopping miserably in a circle of salt, burning sage sticking out of his ragged trousers. She broke into peels of merry laughter when Mrs Dorritt tripped and dumped the bowl of cow's urine she had been carrying so carefully all over his head.

Wiping the tears from her face, Alice brandished the device and declared, "What fun I'm going to have here." As you can imagine, the villagers didn't exactly respond very favourably.'

'I'm not sure who threw the first stone. You have to remember, we had no technology in those days. To my villagers, the 'weapon' that Alice was wielding was akin to the devil. It scared them badly, and they reacted badly.'

'When a pebble hit her cheek, causing the blood to flow, Alice stamped her feet, triggered the device, and tearfully cried out, "Freeze, all of you! I'll make you pay for that."'

'Immediately, everybody stopped mid-motion. Alice meandered over to take a closer look, flicking her finger on Mrs Dorritt's nose as she passed by.'

'"You lot are now mice and…dodos!" she laughed, aiming the device. "Go on, have a race or something."'

'I was later told it was quite chilling to hear her giggle and snigger while watching the villagers stumble in the mud, squeaking and cooing, desperation in their eyes. Rather unhinged, that girl.'

'After some time, Alice grew bored, yawning and looking around for fresh bait. Her eyes fell on Owen, who was sitting outside his house like he normally did on sunny days. He had been watching her thoughtfully, drawing on his pipe and absently stroking the old dog sleeping next to him.'

'"What's so funny about tormenting those poor folk," he drawled in that deep, resonant voice of his. "Don't you have the imagination to think of something better to do?"'

'Alice frowned at the contempt in his voice. "I can imagine plenty, thank you very much," she stated primly, her intense eyes narrowing as she looked at him. "If you're so concerned, why don't you get up and help them? Too frightened?" she jeered.'

'Instead of taking offence, Owen just smiled that easy smile of his and doffed his hat. "Well, little lady. I find it hard to move around these days since the cannonball took these." With that, he swept aside the lap blanket to reveal his wooden legs.'

'Alice's eyes lit up in delight. She ran over and knocked on the gnarled wood. "For luck," she said, flashing her teeth at him. "Where I come from, people usually get robotic replacements, not twigs like those. Curiouser and curiouser! I think I am *very* far from home." Shrugging, she turned away, already losing interest.'

'Quick as a flash, Owen grabbed her wrist and tried to wrestle the device from her hand. Alice lashed out and viciously clawed him across the cheek, her face red and furious.'

'"How dare you," she screamed, spittle flying from her lips. "Nobody is allowed to touch me, not after…" She shuddered, then pushed the trigger. "Crawl, you creep. Crawl like a caterpillar until your hands bleed."'

'Owen sagged to the floor, his eyes boring defiantly into hers. His strong shoulders bunched as they bore the weight of his large, unresisting body and he dragged himself along, old Oscar licking his face in confusion. He winced as one of the villager 'mice' trampled his hand as she scuttled past, squeaking and crying. But he continued to struggle inch by torturous inch towards the tree line, head held proud.'

'Alice watched in satisfaction, a cruel smirk playing about her thin lips. With a toss of her head, she dismissed her shameful act and sniffed the air. Mrs Bradley was making some of her famous soup.'

'Alice wandered towards the delicious smell, nose held high. Stopping by the open window of a small house, she breathed deeply and sighed in satisfaction. "I want some of that," she announced, and banged open the kitchen door.'

'Mrs Bradley gave a small scream of surprise when Alice barged in. She had been busily chopping vegetables and carefully adding spices to the soup, and had no idea of the awfulness outside. "Get out!" she ordered. "Nobody is allowed in here while I'm cooking." She turned away, snorting in disgust. Alice stared at her back, eyes darkening. "Give me food," she demanded quietly, her free hand clenching.'

'Mrs Bradley looked at her in astonishment, quite unused to her authority being challenged in her own kitchen. "Don't you dare take that tone with me, young lady," she warned, waving her spoon in anger. "This soup is for the Lady, not for ragamuffins like you. Go on, get out of here

A Likely Story

now before I do something you'll regret."'

'Alice stood there, gritting her teeth. Then grinned. "That soup is going to need a bit more pepper," she said sweetly, her finger hovering over the trigger.'

'"Don't be ridiculous girl, I've already added some and it's perfect as it is. What a cheek, a snip of a girl like you trying to tell me how to do my job. I've just about had enough." She stalked towards Alice, her spoon raised high, red spots of anger staining her cheeks.'

'Alice laughed and fired. "Add more pepper, little cook," she commanded, pointing at the big tubs of spices proudly displayed on the shelf. "Lots and lots of pepper." She stood back out of range as Mrs Bradley reluctantly picked up the largest tub, lifted the lid, and added a pinch or two to the soup.'

'"Oh come on now, you can do better than that," taunted Alice. "Why not try the whole tub, that'll be nice. Go on, all of it."'

'A tear rolled down Mrs Bradley's cheek as she slowly upended the tub. At first nothing happened, then the pepper succumbed to gravity and fell out of the container in a dense cloud that enveloped the unfortunate woman.'

'What happened next was most unpleasant. My poor cook collapsed into a fit of coughing and sneezing, her eyes and nose red and streaming from the noxious fumes. Alice collapsed into gales of laughter, holding her stomach as she watched the suffering woman roll around the floor, gasping for breath. After some time, her merriment subsided and she skipped over to look down at Mrs Bradley. "I don't think I want any of that soup after all," she mocked. "It's a bit too spicy for me, I'm afraid." She grinned widely at the bloodshot eyes glaring at her and wandered off to find some more amusement.'

'She strolled down the lane, carelessly swinging the device as she walked, distracted by the motes of pollen dancing in the air. She jumped in surprise when a voice hailed her.'

"'Good morning, young miss. Are you lost? I haven't seen your face before. Would you like to join us for a cup of tea and some cake? We love talking to new people." Tom's face beamed at her from the small doorway, surrounded by a spray of pink roses.'

'Her stomach rumbled loudly and she licked her lips. "Yes please," she said politely, no trace of the earlier mischief in her face. "I am so *very* hungry."'

"'Come on in then, my dear," said Tom, standing aside and gesturing to the open door. "You are more than welcome. Our little girl is asleep right now, but I'm sure we won't wake her." He towered over Alice as she entered his home, his prominent teeth shining in his beaming face.'

'Alice smiled at the scene that greeted her. A young woman was pouring tea, while a small child with soft, tumbling curls was slumbering peacefully in the rocking chair. Sunshine streamed through the large window, bathing

A Likely Story

the room in a golden glow, adding to the warmth of the tiny fire crackling in the grate. A plethora of hats covered one wall, while scraps of lace and ribbon and felt covered a large table beneath. The woman looked up and smiled.'

'"Why hello there," she said softly. "What a pleasant surprise. Has Tom been collecting strays again?" Alice scowled at the description, then her face softened as the woman took her gently by the hand and led her to a large, comfortable chair beside the child.'

'"Sit yourself down, take the weight off your feet. My name is Emily, Tom you've already met, and this is Dora, our dozy little dormouse. Please excuse the mess over there. I'm a hat maker, as you can probably guess. I've just finished that beautiful top hat for the Lady's husband. Do you like it?" she asked, pointing to a resplendent black hat. Alice gave a small whistle of appreciation, making Emily smile proudly. "Let me fetch another cup," she said. "And I expect you'd like a sandwich or two?" Alice nodded appreciatively as Emily disappeared into the small kitchen.'

'Sighing in satisfaction, she looked down at the sleeping girl. Her eyes soft and suspiciously bright, she tenderly brushed a stray lock from the delicate cheek. She jolted when Tom broke into her reverie. "Try not to wake her," he admonished. "She was up so very early today and needs her rest."'

'Her face darkening, Alice sat stiff in the chair, the device lying in her lap. As he turned away, she defiantly poked the child, causing her to mumble and stir. Tom turned back quickly, staring hard at Alice who was looking innocently out of the window. A slight crease marred his forehead as he walked over to the window to get a better look at his beautiful, engraved pocket watch. Alice grinned, that troublesome gleam lighting her eyes once more.'

'As Emily bustled back into the room, laden with a tray of sandwiches, cake and an extra cup, Tom hurried over to relieve her. They sat at the dining table and looked at Alice. "Please, join us," said Emily, pointing to the remaining chair. "Plenty to go around."'

'Alice grinned and stood up, giving Dora a quick prod as she moved away. The little girl snorted loudly, making Alice giggle. Tom looked at her, frowning. "I saw that," he said in annoyance. "I'm sure you didn't mean it, but do *not* wake her. Sit down and have a sandwich." Alice sighed petulantly, and wandered over.'

'I think she was already getting tired of the couple's niceness, to be honest. Patience was never her strong point, and she really didn't know how to react normally in social situations. She was itching for excitement.'

'She snatched up an egg sandwich from a china plate and began to roam the room, the device still firmly gripped in her other hand. Emily and Tom looked at each other, eyebrows raised. As she passed the sleeping child again, she kicked the chair, making it rock wildly. Dora half woke and drowsily sang, "Twinkle, twinkle, twinkle, twinkle…", before dozing off once more. "Well really!" said Tom crossly. "What dreadful behaviour, after we were kind enough to ask you to tea."'

'Alice laughed and strode over to Emily's workspace, picking up one fragment of material after another. She knew Emily was becoming agitated behind her, and a smirk twisted her lips. Suddenly, she grabbed the top hat with both hands, scattering egg and breadcrumbs on the brim, and put it on her head. "Does it suit me?" she asked, cocking her head to one side."'

'She relished the look of horror on Emily's face as she dashed over and removed it, lovingly wiping it clean. "Be careful," Emily scolded. "That's a whole month's wages you almost ruined." She carefully set it down on the table, then studied Alice. "And no, it didn't really suit you," she replied. "Your golden hair is beautiful, but it badly needs a good wash and cut before it would be suitable for *my* hats."'

'Alice looked at her, outraged, and triggered the device. "You're so high and mighty, it makes me sick,' she shouted. 'Put that hat on and let's see how perfect *you* look."'

'Surprised, Emily reached over, gently picked up the top hat and set it over her fair curls. "Come on then," goaded Alice. "Carry on lording it over us inferior beings, why don't you." She laughed delightedly as Emily began to strut around the small room, head held high. "I want wine now,' Emily demanded, shaking her finger at an imaginary minion. "In a clean cup, mind, or I'll have your head." She stopped and plucked at the hat. "What is this infernal thing doing here, it's covered in breadcrumbs. Shoddy work." With that, she casually tossed the hat into the fireplace and swaggered off outside.'

'"And as for you," Alice said, whirling to face Tom, who sat unmoving in shock at the sight of all that hard work twisting and burning in the fire. "What do you think of this?" She grabbed the jug of water from the table and threw it over Dora, who woke with a shriek and began to wail loudly, hair dripping into her eyes. Tom's long face flushed deeply, and he bared his large teeth as he lunged across the table to grab Alice. His heavy watch fell out of his pocket and into the full cup of tea. "No!" he cried out. "My Da gave me that before he died. You terrible, terrible girl. Just wait until I get my hands on you." Alice rolled her eyes and raised the device. "Oh, dip it some more, why don't you. I've had enough."'

'"Stupid tea party," she muttered as she stalked out the door and back down the lane, munching on the half-eaten sandwich and leaving the trail of destruction behind her.'

'It was some time before she reached *my* home. We had a long driveway that led through the grounds, and Alice was incredibly tired by the time she reached the beautiful formal gardens. That might have contributed to her terrible behaviour, I don't know.'

'She later told us about her fascination with the flamingo statues framing the ornate garden gates, a gift from my adventurer friend. They were only a fable by the time Alice was born. It seems much of our wildlife had become extinct by then. The incessant drive towards technology had left no room for the natural world. It could have been so different, I'm sure. They could have worked in harmony. But who am I to know, an old woman displaced in time?'

'We were all rather shocked when she stumbled onto my lawn that warm, sunny afternoon. The guards immediately stopped their game of cards (well, it *was* a peaceful place) and advanced towards her, pikes raised. I of course told them to stand down, as I could see that she was ready to fall down. I ordered Wadsworth to bring over a chair and help her sit. He also brought some of my wonderful lemonade, which certainly revived her. I only like to use a small drop of honey to sweeten it.'

'Once she'd finished coughing and spluttering, she sat back to look at me. That was when I first glimpsed those mesmerising eyes and they unnerved me, I must admit. "Thank you," she said, one eyebrow raised. She turned to look at the guards, who were still hovering menacingly nearby. "Are they really necessary?" she asked, waving that strange device at them. Immediately, they raised their pikes defensively. "Oh go away and finish your game of snap," she exclaimed in irritation. "In fact," she added, pressing the trigger. "Use yourself as cards. That would be much more interesting."'

'Immediately, my loyal guards began throwing themselves onto the ground, one on top of the other, each bellowing "Snap!". Every shout was accompanied by the chilling snap of a delicate bone as another heavy body landed on it. Their cries quickly turned to yelps of pain, yet as soon as the bottom man scrambled free, he threw himself back onto the pile. It was pitiful and heart wrenching, and some moments passed before I could react.'

"'Stop!" I implored, turning to the girl. "Please, whatever witchery you are doing, stop it. You'll kill them." I turned to my husband, who finally had trotted out of that blasted study of his to see what "all the darned fuss" was about, and demanded that he go and fetch Dr Moore this instance. He quickly scurried off to carry out my instructions, his short legs pumping like mad.'

'Don't look so surprised. I know I ordered him around a bit. But I was in charge, you know, it was my land after all. And unlike many women in my time, I didn't need a man to tell *me* what to do. Certainly not one like him, always lost in his research and needing me to make all the decisions.'

'In the meantime, Wadsworth had managed to separate the men, who were lying groaning on the immaculate grass, clutching their injured limbs. I was just about to tell him to go and find some splints and bandages, when I heard Alice sigh deeply behind me.'

"'Oh I am so bored by all this fuss," she said, yawning. "Leave those moaning Minnies and let's have a game instead. What about croquet, I've heard of that one. I've always wanted to try it." I looked at her in astonishment, her callous remarks cutting through my worry for the guards. "Don't be ridiculous, girl. These men need help immediately, I can't let them suffer." She simply looked at me and smirked.'

'As she pressed down on the trigger, a most peculiar sensation washed over me. My thoughts became fuzzy and indistinct and I lost all focus. I looked at her and couldn't help but latch on to her every word. "Play croquet with me," she demanded, and suddenly it seemed the most important thing in the world that I should obey her. Without a further thought for my poor guards, I wandered over to the croquet lawn. "We don't have a ball," I muttered dreamily. Wadsworth looked at me in complete astonishment, assuming I'd lost my mind. Which I had, of course, albeit temporarily.'

'Alice ran over to look for a substitute. "This'll do," she declared, handing over a hedgehog rolled up protectively. Rather than protest, I smiled at her obediently and took the poor creature. Ignoring the spikes digging into my palm, I set it on the grass and gently placed my foot on top. Then, and to my everlasting shame, I whacked it as hard as I could with the wooden mallet. I heard Wadworth give a shout of amazement, but it meant nothing to me. I simply watched as Alice rolled on the floor, laughing like crazy.'

'I later realised my actions had tipped my beloved Wadsworth over the edge. He knew I would never condone such behaviour if I was in my right mind. His normally gentle face was suffused with rage as he prowled towards Alice, a spare mallet in his hands. With a profound look of satisfaction, he clouted her on the side of the head as she sat gasping, holding her stomach. She slumped to the ground, her wild hair falling over her face, the device spilling onto the grass. Warily, he approached me, apologising profusely. "I am so, so sorry, my Lady,' he said. "Please forgive me." I stood there in complete unconcern as he knocked me senseless.

'When I came to, Wadsworth was pointing the device at me. "It seems to have a reverse switch, Ma'am," he said. "I'm going to try it and hope that you come back to us." He looked at me for a long moment, in that way that he sometimes did, and activated it.

'It was as though a blanket of fog lifted to clear my mind. Apart from the terrible pounding in my skull, of course. "You might have tried that without knocking me out first," I reproached, touching the lump forming on my head and glaring at him. His face flushed crimson and I relented, gently touching his cheek and leaning closer. "Thank you for saving me, dearest one," I whispered softly, my lips brushing his ear, before returning to my normal, brisk manner.

'"Tie that creature up," I ordered, pointing towards Alice. "Then go and get help for those poor men. Oh, and use the contraption on them first, we don't want any repeats of *that* little performance!" I wheeled around, ready to start wrapping broken bones.'

'To my surprise, a mob of angry villagers was storming

up the driveway, vigorously brandishing all sorts of sharp implements. "Where is she?" they yelled, many with faces and clothes covered in mud and scratches. "Hand over the witch, we'll make her pay for what she did to us."'

'Well, as much as I would have loved to do as they asked, I simply couldn't. I was the highest authority in our little part of the world, and I knew that even *she* should have some justice. So I managed to calm them down, before telling them she would receive a fair trial like anybody else. Right now, in fact.'

'They weren't exactly happy. "Off with her head," I heard someone cry out, pointing at Alice who had recovered her senses. "Hang her high!" called out another. "Burn the witch," was the last exclamation I heard before I raised my hand for peace. My word was law and they reluctantly agreed.'

'And that's how I learned the true extent of her wickedness. My heart hurt for my poor villagers, especially brave Owen who had regained his mind while dragging himself through a bramble bush. It must have taken a long while for those deep wounds to heal, and not just the physical ones. Tom was livid with Alice for the damage to his pocket watch. I'd be surprised if it ever kept good time again.'

'Surprisingly, Emily came to Alice's defence during the trial after hearing her story, despite her own loss. She was always a tender soul, that one, and it broke her heart to hear how Alice had suffered in the institute. It was at that moment, when our guard was lowered and we were beginning to empathise with Alice, that she took her chances and fled, taking the device with her. It took us a long moment before we reacted, and she was halfway down the driveway before we gave chase.'

'We eventually caught up with her, sweating and panting, in the same muddy field in which she'd arrived. We gaped in astonishment at the sight of the glowing hole still suspended in the air, and nervously backed away. Alice simply laughed and strolled nearer to the curious sight.'

'"It's magical, isn't it,' she said, waving towards the hovering shimmer. "I'm hoping it will take me to a different wonderland this time. I've had quite enough of you lot, that's for sure. Very rude, some of you. Especially that knave over there." She glared at Wadsworth, who took a step towards her. "Stay right there," she warned, raising the device. "Or I'll use this on you one last time and leave you grubbing in the mud like the animals you are." He stared angrily at her, but edged back a little.'

'While she had been talking, I had been sidling closer around the back of the crowd, my shorter height hiding me from view. I refused to let her escape justice, and was intent on recapturing her. I had just managed to come within grabbing distance when she noticed me.'

'"No, no, little Queenie. You won't be catching me again. This little Alice is too clever for the likes of you. Ta ta for now!" And with that, she dived into the hole.'

'Stupidly, without a second thought for the inevitable consequences, I clutched the leg that was disappearing fast and held on tight. My last memory of that wonderful life was the sound of Wadsworth screaming out my name, before the hole snapped shut.'

'The rest is history, so to speak. I ended up here in this miserable place, lost and alone and completely bewildered. In fact, I have a little more sympathy for Alice now, after my spell in the psychiatric unit. It took me a long while to realise that people would never believe my story. When they eventually let me out I ended up here, and I've been slaving away ever since.'

'I've lived with the pain of losing my little boy for so long now. I do miss him so very much. And my dearest Wadsworth, I am lost without him. They're both long dead now, of course.'

'I suppose I shouldn't forget my husband — although I bet he quickly forgot about me. It was no secret he much preferred his damnable experiments. I often wonder whether he had any children of his own, it would have been a shame for that incredible knowledge to be lost. What's that, you have your suspicions? Hmm, he always did like that chambermaid a little *too* much. I wouldn't be surprised if she ended up carrying his child.'

'Well, lunch is over, I'm afraid. I can see my boss is getting annoyed, and my story is done. I'd say it's been nice talking to you, but the memories are too painful. I don't know what you can do with them though. Take it from me, nobody will ever believe you if you try and tell the truth. Best to go back to your own life and forget about it, dear. Goodbye. And don't forget to pay your bill on the way out.'

LOCKED AWAY

'I am Dr Gothel, sit there please. I have precious little time to spare and my patients are waiting. How may I help you?'

'Yes, I suppose this room is rather bleak. But what do you expect? I *am* running an asylum, not one of those newfangled hotels. Although there was talk of King George staying with us for a while, his mind isn't what it used to be. Maybe I should add a picture or two…?'

'Sorry, I digress. What was so urgent that I had to break from my rounds to speak to you?'

'Why of course I remember Alice. She is not an easy woman to forget. May I ask about your interest in her, are you a relation?'

'I see. Well, I'm not at all surprised she caused your friend some distress. Her mind worked rather differently to ours, she was tainted by wildness. She certainly turned this place upside down. However, I really can't tell you what happened if you are not family, so I must ask you to leave.'

'What do you mean, you'll tell everyone my secret if I don't talk? I am quite sure I don't know what you're referring to, young lady, but I don't like your tone. Please stop wasting my time and get out.'

'How dare you, I am a man of honour. I would never continue to claim money from our charity for women who've run away. What a scandalous idea. I've a good mind to call my guards and take you for assessment, you have clearly lost your mind.'

'There is no use trying to blackmail me. My books are in perfect order. So unless you have anything more substantial than wild speculation, I must ask you to leave.'

'Wh…where did you get these papers? They're from my private collection, nobody could have known where I hid them. Have you been spying on me? What do you want, money? How much will stop you telling my employers about my…misappropriation?'

'Is that *really* all you want, the story behind that troubled woman? Why is she so important that you're willing to ruin my career unless I talk?'

'Fine, so be it. But be warned…if you ever return, I will have you locked away in a cell so deep, you will *never* see the light of day again.'

'We found Alice wandering the grounds in the depths of the night, one bitterly cold winter. Josef, the nightguard, had stumbled into my quarters, babbling about a shimmering hole in the sky and a pale white ghost that had emerged to haunt the rose bushes.'

'Quite preposterous, of course, and I told him as much as I marched outside in my dressing gown to see what all the fuss was about. I fully expected that one of my girls had escaped again, and I was determined to discover how they were getting through locked doors.'

'Only I had the keys to each room, you see. Yet they were still managing to slip away. The situation was becoming untenable and my reputation was at stake. Although my bank balance *had* become somewhat larger as a result...'

'We made our way past the kitchen gardens and down into the dormant rose maze. As we passed under the arched entrance, I saw a strange woman dressed in a white garment that floated on the night breeze, her halo of golden hair shining in the pale moonlight. I must admit, even my heart skipped a beat at her wraithlike appearance.'

'I approached cautiously, not wanting to scare her. My patients were easily disturbed, especially at night, and I didn't want to rouse them into a frenzy if they woke up. As I drew closer, I saw a faint, secretive smile curl her lips as she slowly blinked at me. The hairs on my neck prickled in response.'

'"Am I home?" she asked gently, her words laced with some deeper emotion I couldn't yet recognise. Her eyes narrowed as she looked up at the large, imposing building. "Yes," she whispered, half to herself. "I do believe am." She looked at me and sighed deeply. "Take me to my room and let me rest," she said tiredly. "And then you can carry on with your damned experiments." I looked at her in confusion, then cursed quietly as she swooned onto the frosty grass.'

'As ever, Josef was quick to rush to the girl's aid, picking up the lithe figure in his strong arms. His tender concern when dealing with our residents was often a source of amusement among the other guards. Most of them were little more than thugs, you understand. It is decidedly hard to find decent men to look after these poor, broken minds. Josef was one of the good ones, and I was thankful to have him as he carried the girl up the countless flights of stairs.'

'Only the tower room was free that night. Despite many girls going missing, we were always being sent more. I sometimes wonder if men simply wanted to rid themselves of unwanted burdens. It is surprisingly easy to find yourself locked up here, if you are a woman. *Imaginary female troubles* or *jealousy* are the most common ailments that seem to afflict our residents, according to the men who send them to us. I do what I can, but I am not entirely surprised so many try to escape.'

'Josef puffed his way up the final few steps as I unlocked the heavy wooden door. Despite the cold wind that whistled through the wooden shutters, I had no choice but to use this one remaining room. While Josef laid the girl on the hard, narrow bed, I went to retrieve several thick blankets from the storeroom below.'

'I returned with my arms laden to find the girl wrapped in Josef's embrace. "Josef!" I exclaimed, shocked by his lack of decorum. "Unhand that girl immediately." He smoothed a golden strand of hair from the pale face. "She was freezing almost to death Doctor," he said quietly, looking at me reproachfully. "I couldn't let her suffer." I rolled my eyes and sighed. "Well, you can let her go now," I replied, walking over to wrap the unconscious girl.'

'"Make sure those shutters are locked tight," I ordered, as I checked the girl for any obvious signs of injury. He stretched his tired arms and rose from the bed. With a final, lingering look at the still shape now covered in blankets, he took out a set of keys and secured the wooden boards.'

'"We will leave the girl in peace,' I stated, after deciding the girl was simply exhausted and cold. "Bring her some food and water and leave it through the slot, as usual. We'll see how she feels in the morning. I want to know how she ended up in our rose garden." With that, I relocked the tower door and we descended to the main building.

'I began to feel drowsy as we entered the relative warmth of the central corridor. "Continue with your rounds, Josef," I said, stifling a yawn. He nodded, and I watched for a moment as he strolled away, opening the small panels in every door to check on the sleeping residents within. Satisfied, I wandered back to my waiting bed.'

'When I checked on our visitor the next morning, she was already awake, pressing her nose against the shutter to sniff the cold morning air. She turned as I entered, and gazed at me for some time before speaking. "You are not my doctor," she said, dismissing me before turning back to the window. I stood for a moment, wondering how to proceed, then slowly picked up a heavy blanket discarded on the bed. "Here you go my dear," I said, approaching slowly to wrap it around her thin shoulders. Her eyes widened for a moment, surprised. Then she blinked and gave a small smile of thanks that quickly disappeared.'

'I stepped back to give her some space. "Can you tell me your name?" I asked. She looked at me in confusion. "Why, Alice, of course," she said. "You surely can't have forgotten me already, I haven't been gone that long." It was my turn to feel bewildered, and I gestured for her to sit down. "We have never met before. We found you wandering the grounds late last night, almost freezing to death. Your poor feet looked quite blue." She looked down at her rather muddy toes and smiled.'

'"I had such fun," she said wistfully. "But Queenie ruined it all and I had to leave. You will have me back, won't you?" I sighed, wondering what to do with her, then offered her my hand. "Josef will draw you a hot bath before his shift ends. We'll find you some warm clothes and get a hot meal inside you. Then you can tell me about yourself and how you ended up here. Does that sound good to you?" She looked at me, eyes shining, and my heart skipped a beat as her soft, slender fingers entwined in mine. Skin tingling, I smiled as I led her downstairs to find Josef.'

'At first, my intention was simply to offer her refuge. I watched her face closely while she told me some of her story, absorbed by her expressive lips and the animation in those astonishing green eyes when relating certain, rather cruel, events. My breath quickened whenever she laid her hand on my arm, the warmth making my pulse race. As the torrent of words slowed, I moved away to stand in the cool breeze from the open window, trying to compose myself.'

'Yet despite my strange fascination with her, I was worried by her bizarre tale and somewhat repulsed by her evident delight at the suffering of others. She seemed quite unaware that her reactions were peculiar. I believed she had the potential to become dangerous, and told myself that I would need to assess her further. For her own safety, I decided to commit her into my care and locked her back into the tower room.'

'She was quite unconcerned by her fate, strengthening my belief that she needed help. She seemed familiar with the routine of an asylum, but was often confused. "Have I returned to my past, which was in the future?" she asked me one day. "Or am I still in my future, which is in the past?" I hardly knew how to respond, instead adding her remark to the already copious notes I had made in her report, to be shared with my benefactors.'

'She genuinely believed she was from the far future, you see. An imaginary place, of course, created to help her mind cope with her problems. She would describe strange metal contraptions that flew through the air, carrying their passengers with them. And a wondrous web that magically connected the whole world and contained all the information you needed, accessed simply by speaking to it. I could have listened for hours as she described the incredible things her mind had invented.'

'But her darker side often showed through, conjuring tales of horror. In her previous life, before her encounter with the 'Queen', she said she had lived in a big house with lots of other young people. Even though they had been taken from their parents, they were mostly happy. Until the men took them to a white, bright room and…'

'She refused to speak for some time after that. She eventually told me they hurt her mind when she wouldn't do what they wanted, 'zapping' her until she fell unconscious. Her exact words, but I had no real idea what she meant.'

'"They wanted to make mindless drones that would obey every order," she whispered during one of our sessions. War was raging across the continents and they were running out of people to send to their deaths. It seemed peace wasn't an option, so they decided to create perfect soldiers to end the fighting. She was one of their first test subjects, she confided, trembling in what I thought was fear.'

'I later realised it was anger. When I laid a soothing hand on her back, shaking slightly at the contact, she told me not to worry, they couldn't hurt her anymore. She had dealt with them all. I dread to think what was in her mind as she spoke, her beautiful face twisted in rage. It may have been a fantasy, but she fully believed it. She stole their device when she escaped and used it on the Queen. Rather conveniently, she lost it when she travelled through the curious hole that had brought her here.'

'Her words startled me, remembering Josef's ramblings about a hole in the sky when we first found her. I determined to have a word with him as soon as possible.'

'To be honest, I had become concerned by his behaviour towards Alice. I knew only too well the allure of the girl, but was determined not to give in to temptation. I wasn't so sure that Josef had resisted.'

'The true extent of their relationship become apparent a short time before he had his…accident.'

'From the outset, Alice had him bewitched. Her evident vulnerability touched his tender heart, but those big soulful eyes undid him. He would visit her often, creeping up the tower stairs whenever he had a moment free, simply to watch her through the small grille in the door.'

'To begin with, she was unaware that he was lurking in the shadows, entranced as she softly sang to herself. One day, she heard the door creak as he leaned closer to hear her lilting refrain. A fleeing glimpse of his dark curly hair as he moved quickly from view made her pause. Her lips curled in amusement as she resumed singing and sauntered over to the window.'

'The beautiful melody ended as she wistfully sighed. "Oh how I wish these shutters could be opened, I do so miss the morning sunshine." Josef bit his lip and fiddled with the window keys attached to his pocket. "I would do anything to be free again," she added, listening to the scuffle of feet as he debated what to do. "Here miss, take this," he eventually said, his voice made hoarse by nervousness. His hand shook as he held the key through the iron grille.'

'Although he saw the exultant smile that flashed across her face as she turned towards him, he was immediately distracted by the adorable look of gratitude that followed. "Would you really be so kind as to give me that key?" whispered Alice. She stepped over to take his big, warm hand in hers. He shivered as she lightly ran her fingers up his muscled forearm.'

'"Goodness, you're a strong man. And gentle, to help a woman like me. I am forever in your debt," she promised, lightly pressing her lips against his skin and thereby sealing his doom. She took the key and went to fling wide the shutters. He sighed deeply, his heart already aching.'

'He talked with her often after that. She kept the key and would sit in the pool of golden sunshine that streamed through the window as they spoke. One day, enticed by a stray lock escaping her cotton cap, he asked her to let down her hair so he could see her full beauty. Normally, we shaved every woman to prevent lice. But Alice refused and instead insisted on washing her hair in lemon water every day to make it shine.'

'With a teasing smile, she slowly removed the cap and shook out her long curls, gazing deep into his eyes. He gulped and licked his suddenly dry lips. "I have to leave," he mumbled, whirling down the stairs before his emotions could betray him further.'

'He took to calling her Rapunzel, after the bellflower that Alice loved so much to eat. Naturally, we take good care of our residents and our kitchen gardens are well stocked with all kinds of foods to nourish the body *and* mind. Josef made sure to slip her some of the slightly bitter herb at every meal, her secret smile of thanks warming his blood.'

'Of course, he couldn't ignore the outbursts of cruelty that Alice often displayed, especially when interacting with other inmates. I remember one occasion when she was playing with a large beetle crawling across the dining table. I'm not ashamed to admit that her look of delight as she casually crushed its head chilled me to the core. It was a bright, sunny day and the iridescent green shell reflected the beams flooding the hall. Turning it this way and that, she sat almost spellbound by the small patch of light dancing amongst the large pewter jugs of icy water.'

'Then she noticed poor Esme staring in wonder, and a particularly cruel smirk twisted her lips. She knew how terribly Esme had suffered at the hands of her father, breaking her fragile mind. She leaned closer, giggling to see the terrified girl shrink away. "It's an angel," she whispered softly. "It's here to protect you…if you can catch it."'

'My heart almost broke to see the look of hope on Esme's face as she scrambled across the table. Her triumph quickly turned to confusion as the golden spot suddenly darted further away. She clambered across the wooden surface, pushing aside plates and spoons and tipping jugs, desperate for salvation. I shouted for the guards to take control and tried to calm the wet, agitated inmates. Alice's merry laughter at the chaos mingled with the screams and yelps of the women around her and the plaintive cries of Esme as she tried to capture her angel.'

'Josef saw the whole sorry event, and others. Yet he still couldn't resist his attraction to her. One day, he made the fateful decision to take the relationship further.'

'When I make my rounds on one of the floors, I leave the other door keys safely locked away – or so I thought. Little did I realise that Josef knew exactly where I kept them and had already made copies for many rooms. Despite the risks should he be found out, his compassion for the women's plight had driven him to set them free.'

'So it was that he decided to help Alice. Although this

time, other emotions besides pity were compelling him to act. He crept up to my office one afternoon while I was on a lower floor, carefully pressed the tower room key into a bar of soap to form an impression, then made a copy filed from a scrap piece of metal.'

'After that, it was relatively simple to spend time wrapped in each other's arms, whispering seductively throughout the night, the fresh spring breeze from the open window cooling hot skin. Their tryst might never have been discovered if it hadn't been for Alice's seeming naivety.'

'With hindsight, Josef had been behaving strangely for some time. He often interacted with the girls, teasing them to make them laugh so they could forget their troubles for a moment or two. Yet he went out of his way to avoid Alice, despite her giving amused looks from under those long lashes. I didn't think too much of it, to be honest, busy as I was documenting her fascinating mind.'

'I finally discovered the truth one day after I told her I needed to move her to another asylum. As ever, I had spent much of our session trying to stop myself gazing at her like a callow youth while she revealed her life as she perceived it. She had become almost an obsession over the last few months, and the constant struggle not to reveal the true depth of my feelings was wearing me down. I knew I had to do something before I behaved unprofessionally.'

'After I broke the news, she looked at me in concern, then closed her eyes. A solitary tear squeezed through her closed lids as she wept. A wild hope that she was upset at the thought of losing me made my heart thump faster. I sat beside her and tentatively put my arm around her hunched shoulders. Resisting the urge to pull her into my lap and hug her to me, I asked her what was wrong.'

'"Oh Dr Gothel, are you sending me away because I am becoming too fat? All of my clothes are too tight and no longer fit me. I have been craving more and more Rapunzel, and Josef has been helping to satisfy me. Am I in trouble because of it?" I frowned as she rubbed her hand over her slightly distended abdomen, and a terrible suspicion began to dawn.'

'I stood quickly, mind whirling. I did catch a glimpse of the strange, crafty look she gave me, but dismissed it in my agitation and ordered her to lie down. Taking out my stethoscope, a relatively new device that my colleague in France had sent to me, I gently pressed it against her abdomen, listening carefully. To my dismay, alongside the strong, steady whoosh of her own heart, I could hear another faint but regular beating. For a moment I stood there with my eyes closed and head hanging, broken-hearted.'

'After a few piteous moments, I let out a deepfelt sigh, gave a wry smile and held out my hand. "You are going to have a baby, Alice," I said gently, not wanting to frighten her. "I won't send you to another asylum, but I will be sending you to a convent so they can look after you both properly." I couldn't help but notice the look of worry that crossed her face, wincing slightly as her grip tightened. I ploughed onwards. "For now, I will move you to another room that is less cold and draughty, this one is no good for you or the baby."'

'Wistfully, I touched her soft cheek, then straightened and guided her out of the room and down into one of the lower cells. I left her perched on the low bed, the weak sunbeams from the small, high window barely piercing the dim room. Eyes wide, she unconsciously rubbed her belly as she watched me close the door with more force than was strictly necessary.'

'I couldn't find it in my heart to be too angry with Alice. She was a disturbed woman who had clearly tried to find solace wherever she could. But my goodness, I was furious with Josef. I suspected he had been rather *too* friendly with an inmate this time. I was almost incandescent with rage, yet it was a cold fury – I have always been a steady man, not one to let my emotions to get the better of me. Part of me wanted to beat the man senseless, but I knew I would need evidence that he had wickedly taken advantage of one my innocent girls. I decided to trap him and catch him in the act.'

'Later that evening, I locked myself into the tower room and flung open the shutters. It was a moonless night, the clouds obscuring any light that might give me away. I lay on the bed and covered myself, hoping the heavy blankets would disguise my bulk, their warmth making me drowsy. While I waited for Josef to appear, I amused myself by pondering a suitable punishment for his shameful deeds.'

'Near midnight, I heard a scuffle on the stairs. My pulse quickened at the scrape of an ill-fitting key being put into the lock. I readied myself as the door opened and heavy footsteps drew near.'

'"Alice, my love, 'tis me. Sorry I am so late. Time has truly dragged today, old Gothel made me do all kinds of unsavoury work." My jaw tightened at being called old, but I smiled in satisfaction to hear his displeasure. In my defence, the latrines had needed a good clean. "Alice?" he said again when I didn't respond, tugging gently at the blankets. "Come here my beauty, give your beloved Josef a kiss."'

'His honeyed words grated my ears and I slowly sat up, savouring the look of horror that broke across his handsome face. "No," he whispered, stepping back until he reached the windowsill. "This can't be happening. What have you done with my Alice? I won't let anyone else hurt her, do you hear me? She's mine." He looked at me in disgust. "She told me the way you kept looking at her. It's pathetic, a man of your age. Do you honestly think a fine woman like that would want an old scrote like you?"'

'I was quite taken aback by the jealousy and anger that coursed through my body at his words. "You have lost her, you villain. You have lost that beautiful girl and you will never see her again," I roared, my face flooding with rage. Overcome, I flung myself at him, my admittedly considerable weight making him stumble. To my horror, he lost his balance and toppled backwards over the narrow ledge. Desperately, I reached out to grab him, but to no avail. I watched in dread as he tumbled through the sky and landed on the thick thorn bushes below.'

'There isn't much left to say after that. Incredibly, he survived the fall with just a few broken bones. But the enormous thorns had pierced his eyes, blinding him instantly. We had to remove them both, winding a cloth around his head to hide the horror of the ragged holes that remained. Not once did he speak while I cared for his wounds, not even to ask about Alice. He simply sat and brooded in silence whenever I was near. He scared me badly.'

'As for Alice, I arranged to send her to the convent as soon as possible. Rather cowardly, I never told her about Josef – and was even less inclined to tell her he was recovering in the next cell. But she somehow discovered the truth, and managed to slip him a message. As I was tending to him one day, I noticed a small smile form on his face, the first sign of emotion he had displayed since his accident. I rewound the bandage, frowning, then jumped violently when his fingers closed around my arms, the nails digging in deep. Sweat dripped down my face as I tried to escape his iron-like grip, and I drew a deep breath to call for help. Suddenly, his grasp loosened, his hands falling back into his lap. Rubbing at my bruised skin, I backed away and hurriedly left the room, deciding to let one of the other guards tend him in future.'

'That guard managed to extract the full details of his bond with Alice, in fact, which he promptly related to me after greasing his palms with a coin or two. In disgust, I gave Josef some money once his limbs had healed, and threw him onto the streets to fend for himself.'

'Alice left not long after. As I guided her to the waiting carriage, her increasing bulk making her somewhat ungainly, she stopped and looked deep into my eyes. "Josef may forever live in darkness, but I will light up his life. Not even you, with your cold, calculating intellect, can keep true love apart. Something you will never experience." With that, she swept past me and climbed into the coach, refusing to look at me further. My heart splintered to watch her being driven away and out of my life.'

'She escaped on the way, of course. The driver stopped deep in the woods to avoid running over the tall, blind beggar standing in the middle of the track. Despite the other man's infirmity, the driver was overcome, tied up and sent on his way in the carriage. Alice disappeared with the beggar into the forest. I have since heard many tales about the blind man and mad woman raising their twins in the wilderness. If they truly did survive, I wish them well. They no longer visit my nightmares, I am thankful to say.'

'So there you have it. A sorry, tawdry tale I'm afraid. Surely not worth all the effort you have clearly gone to, but that was our bargain. Please, hand over those papers and leave. I never want to see your face again, beautiful as it is. I've had enough of that kind of beauty to last me a lifetime. Leave me in peace, so I can tend to the girls that still need me. At least *they* are grateful that I am looking after them.'

'Go on, get out! My guards would be only too happy to take care of you. Do you want me to call them? Hmm, I thought not. Shut the door behind you. And remember…do *not* show your face here ever again.'

A PESKY PROBLEM

'Come here little ratty, look what I've got for you. This lovely bit of cheese is much better than the rubbish you'll find in this awful place. Come on little one, let me take you somewhere safe.'

'Oh my goodness me, you made me jump. Where on earth did *you* spring from? Sneaking around like that is not a good idea, young lady. I would never hurt you, of course, I *am* a man of God. But others aren't so law-abiding, not in this town anyway.'

'You've been searching for me, have you? Not another rat problem, they're running wild at the moment. Let me finish up here and I'll soon sort you out. Here, ratty, come to papa.'

'You're *not* here about the rats? Well, I haven't got much else to talk about, to be honest. I keep myself to myself, you know. Everybody seems to want my services, but nobody at all wants my company.'

'Oh, it's okay, I'm used to it. Catching these so-called filthy vermin was never going to be socially acceptable, I knew that when I started. But rats are such intelligent creatures, and I abhor violence. I can't bear to see them killed simply for trying to eat.'

'When I left the monastery at Hamelin, I made it my life's work to look after these poor creatures. I catch them alive and release them into the wild. I love my work, I really do. I don't need the folks around here, their conversation isn't the most stimulating, I'm afraid. I'm far happier with my beloved rats and my bible. Sometimes I can sit for hours, playing songs to them on my pipe. They seem to be entranced by the melodies. People laugh when they hear me piping to the rats, but I don't care.'

'Let me introduce you to my friend, Dougal. Look, there he is, his little nose is poking out of my pocket. Stroke his coat, feel how soft and silky it is. Don't be afraid, my dear, he won't bite.'

'There's no need to shudder quite so much, he *is* harmless you know. And very intelligent indeed, I've taught him to do several tricks. I'm sure he would be quite offended if he could understand you. I've had to put this yellow ribbon round his neck because of people's fear of this innocent creature. He's escaped a few times and I've discovered people are less likely to kill what is clearly a pet than a wild rodent. Even if it *is* trying to steal your food.'

'I can see you're just like the rest, repelled by the mere

thought of a rat. Here, sit down for a moment, take the weight off your feet. Tell me, if rats aren't invading your home, how can *I* possibly help?'

'You want to know more about the story of the rat catcher and the missing children? My goodness me, I'm surprised anyone beyond our town walls has heard about *that* little saga. As a matter of fact, I *did* rid the town of them. Not that anyone was particularly grateful. They don't shun me quite like they used to, but they're certainly rather wary of me now. A slight improvement, I suppose.'

'How did I do it? I'm not sure I should tell you. If Father Conall was to hear about it, he would denounce me for consorting with the devil. And you're not likely to believe my tale anyway.'

'Nothing will surprise you anymore, eh? Well…okay then. Sit back, have some of this water, and listen carefully. But don't say I didn't warn you!'

'It all began several years ago. I had just left the sanctuary of the monastery to follow my vocation. Hamelin had recently become a town, and the rats were out of control. I soon learned that I would never be short of money – most of which I send back to Father Conall, of course. And I very quickly realised that my learning compared to these…yokels meant that I would never fit in with their simple way of life. Despite my efforts to educate them, they seemed to hold me in some contempt.'

'Arrogant, me? I hardly think so. I am simply far more learned and, if I'm honest, intelligent. I'm quite sure that has nothing to do with the way they treat me, thank you very much. May I continue?'

'One morning, I was strolling along the track through the woods to the town. I live outside the boundary walls, you should know. A simple dwelling on the edge of a small farm. Peace and quiet, and a place to escape from the dirt of the streets and the bovine stares of the townsfolk. The baker had developed a terrible rat problem, and they were nibbling at his morning bread. I was wondering how best to remove them when a glowing circle appeared in the sky.'

'Naturally, I fell to my knees in awe and terror. Surely this was God appearing to his most loyal and humble servant? I gazed at the shimmering apparition, before hanging my head and praying fervently in case this was my last moment on earth.'

'As I knelt in supplication, a whooshing noise alerted me to a projectile flying through the air. Before I could react, it whacked me on the temple, knocking me out cold.'

'It was some time before I regained my senses. Carefully rubbing the throbbing lump on my head, I sat up and looked around. My heart sank when I realised the holy vision had disappeared. Sighing, I climbed to my feet and tried to see what had hit me.'

'To my surprise, a small metallic object lay nearby in the lush, green grass. I stepped over to examine it more closely.

I had never seen the like before, and its unnatural design unnerved me. Guessing it could be dangerous, I decided not to leave it lying around.'

'Gingerly, I wrapped my hands around the device. It felt strangely warm, sitting heavy on my palm, and a couple of depressions marred its smooth surface. I resisted the temptation to press them, and slipped it into my pocket. Vowing to look at it the moment I returned home, I continued my journey to work.'

'I was just putting the finishing touches to my rat trap, coughing in the flour dust that coated every surface, when Riff walked in. My spirits plummeted, knowing there was only one reason the bane of my life would be there.'

'"Oh look, it's little Aldred, the rat lover," he jeered, thumbs hooked casually in the pockets of his jerkin. He walked over and kicked my carefully prepared trap. I grit my teeth and prayed for patience.'

'"What do you want, Riff?" I asked somewhat testily as I reset the trap. "Shouldn't you be fixing that wall for Mistress Brunhilde? She won't be pleased to find you slacking again." I looked up, unsurprised to see the anger flash across his wide, brutish face. Even the most innocent remarks were enough to set him off.'

'Breathing heavily, he grabbed my hair. "I don't like you Aldred, always thinking you're better than the rest of us. I think it's time someone taught you a lesson." With that, he hauled me to my feet and pressed me against the wall, his hot, stinking breath blasting in my face.'

'As he jostled me, that strange device fell out of my pocket and clattered to the floor. Surprised, he bent for a closer look, still holding his hand tight around my throat.'

'"Well then," he drawled, turning the smooth metal over in his meaty palm. "What is our Aldred up to now, I wonder? Looks mighty suspicious, does this. Must be worth a fortune, it's crafted so well. Who did you steal it from, rat boy?" He flexed his fingers, making me choke, and my eyes bulged as I struggled for air. Reluctantly, he released his grip to let me speak.'

'I leaned over for a moment, gasping and thinking quickly. I knew the device wasn't for the likes of Riff. It was a gift from God, and I wanted to take it to Father Conall for safekeeping. "Look, I'll show you what it does," I promised, knowing he wasn't too bright. With a shrug, he handed it to me. "No tricks," he warned, sneering at my evident fear.'

'Taking a deep breath, I held the object tightly in my hands then decided to make a run for it. Like my beloved rats, I could be fleet-footed when needed and easily slipped past Riff's protruding stomach. But his large frame belied his speed and he grabbed the back of my tunic before I could make it to the door. Shouting in fear as he spun me round, I accidentally pressed one of the indentations. "Stop," I cried. "You're hurting me, you pig."'

'To my utmost surprise, he dropped to his knees and

began rooting around the dusty floor, squealing and grunting. I stared at him in astonishment, sure he had lost his mind. Then I looked at the device and began to wonder.'

'Despite my growing fear, curiosity got the better of me and I pressed the button again. "Sit still," I commanded, and jumped when Riff immediately sat and crossed his legs, quietly snuffling.'

'I leaned against a sack of flour and wiped away the sweat trickling down my neck. Heart racing, I thought about what this could mean. A device capable of controlling someone's mind was most likely ungodly. I decided to try it once more. "Lie down and roll over," I demanded, hand shaking slightly as I aimed at Riff.'

'Revenge? Why, the thought never crossed my mind, especially using that accursed tool. What a terrible thing to suggest, such behaviour is beneath a man of God like myself. I've a good mind not to carry on.'

'Ouch, your nails are rather sharp. Let go of my arm, I'll finish my tale.'

'Riff fell heavily to one side and began rolling around the floor. Despite myself, I began to chuckle as he turned white in the churning clouds of flour. The giggles died when I saw the look of hatred burning from his small, pale eyes. Somewhat alarmed, I told him to stop and sit quietly.'

'Clearly, that infernal contraption could cause great harm if it fell into the wrong hands. I was even more determined to take it to Father Conall. Using it one last time,

I gave my final commands to Riff. "You *will* forget all about this," I ordered. "And you will never bother me again," I added as an afterthought.'

'No, I didn't feel particularly guilty controlling him that way. We might have been taught never to impose our will on others, but I was so weary of his constant taunts and threats. Even a meek man like myself has limits, you know, and I felt sure God would forgive me.'

'Nevertheless, I pledged never to use it again, and meant every word. Until that fateful time when the town fell into great danger and I had no other choice.'

'I spent several months in relative peace, the device slipping from my mind. I had hidden it in a safe place near my home, secure until I had chance to visit Father Conall. Riff certainly never bothered me again, and for that I was eternally grateful. I had time to work and study, and life was good. But then the young gangs began to terrorise our lives.'

'Our town had been devastated after the uprising against the Bishop, some two decades ago. Times were hard, and many had succumbed to hunger and deprivation while trying to rebuild. As is ever the case with us humans, others had seized the opportunity to grow rich and fat by exploiting their fellow men. Those who suffered the most were the poor orphaned children, used like slaves in the pursuit of wealth. Like I said, we all have limits and eventually the children rebelled.'

'Unknown to us, they had begun to meet secretly, dreaming up ways to make their lives more bearable. They had lived alongside the power of money all of their short, miserable lives, but had only experienced the helplessness of poverty. They knew which they preferred.'

'So they began to steal. Small items at first, the odd wallet here or small purse there. As they grew more successful and became acquainted with a full belly at every meal, the crimes began to escalate. Soon, even the smallest of them became adept at sneaking up behind their victim and threatening to stab them if they didn't hand over their valuables. Their network of spies and fellow thieves allowed them to escape with their ill-gotten gains and quickly disappear into the murkier districts of town.'

'The council tried to flush them out, of course. And they did manage to capture one or two, I believe. But they never ratted – so to speak – on the gang, despite their severe punishment. The thieving little guttersnipes remained free to wreak perilous havoc on upstanding citizens.'

'At least, that is how they were described at the large town meeting one night, when Burgermeister Hass had finally had enough after being sliced through the back of the leg by one young thief. From his description, I believe the small boy could have been no more than six years of age. But to hear our esteemed leader talk, the child was a feral animal out to kill him.'

'Hass was certainly adept at whipping up anger and

turmoil. In his loud, booming voice, he reminded the packed room of the injustices carried out by these ungrateful, savage urchins – neglecting to mention the hardships that each and every child had suffered, often at his own hands. The people became angrier and more agitated, demanding a solution to rid the town of the brats.'

'A workcamp was suggested, but quickly discarded after realising they would have to part with their own money to maintain it. But the crowd roared their approval when poison was put forward as the most humane (and, of course, cheapest…) option. "The children have suffered enough," it was argued. "Let's put them out of their misery, so that we can go back to keeping our own families safe. Nobody will ever miss them, after all."'

'I was horrified, of course. I couldn't even condone the killing of rats, let alone these poor unwanted children. Outraged, I demanded to be heard.'

'They were reluctant to let a mere rat catcher have a say in important business, until I reminded them that I was still a servant of God. "Suffer the little children," I cautioned. "That was his instruction to us. We can't go around killing them simply because they're inconvenient. They deserve a better life, not a death sentence. Let *me* deal with the problem, I can handle it."'

'"How is a miserable wretch like you going to do that?" demanded Hass. "You might be good at catching rats, but even *these* little imps are more intelligent. They'll easily outwit you." I reassured the room that I had a plan, and they reluctantly agreed to give me a week. "Make sure you succeed," warned Hass. "Because if you don't, *you* will be the one to secure the poison and carry out the task. I'm sure you have easy access, considering your…trade," he added disdainfully. I shuddered and left the room, deep in thought.'

'Truth was, I had no real idea how to catch the children. There were so many of them and too wily for me to trap alone. I went back to my house to form a plan.'

'It wasn't until later that evening, while I was watching Dougal roll around on the dusty floor in play, that I remembered Riff. A shiver ran up my spine as I began to wonder if the device could help me. It may have been an abominable instrument, but surely God would prefer me to use that than let the children die. But would it work on more than one person at once? I fell into a troubled sleep, determined to experiment with it the next day.'

'With Dougal secure in one big pocket and the device clasped tightly in the other, I marched down an alleyway that I knew the children frequented. I had decided to perform a little show, with Dougal as the star. Heavens knew that these children rarely had any entertainment, only sorrow, so I felt sure I would get a small audience. And then I could see if they could all be controlled at once.'

'Finding a relatively clean spot, I placed the board I had been carrying on top of an old abandoned barrow and set up the little course I had devised for Dougal. From the corner of my eye, I could see two little heads peering from a broken window. I carried on, giving no hint that I had seen them.'

'Once the items were ready, I put a small cube of cheese at one end, then released Dougal into the other. He knew the score, and quickly scurried over and through the obstacles, nose twitching and squeaking slightly in excitement. As he worked his way through the course, I played a lively little melody on my pipe. I smiled to see two children warily creeping closer to get a better look, eyes wide in delight. As I watched them, the idea of killing little ones like this struck me as truly monstrous. I quickly swallowed the lump in my throat as tears burned my eyes.'

'Dougal reached the cheese, as he always managed to do, and I reset the course in a different layout. "What do you think?" I whispered to the children, so as not to alarm them. "Will Dougal reach the cheese *this* time?" They looked up at me, wide grins on their faces. "Yes!" one whispered back, careful not to frighten Dougal. "He's so clever, he could do anything." I winked at him, then set Dougal free.'

'As they eagerly watched Dougal's every move, I stealthily swapped my pipe for the device and aimed it at them. "You will listen to me, and listen quietly," I commanded, then fired. Both children stared up at me, Dougal quite forgotten as he nibbled on his cheesy prize. I stared back, somewhat amazed that it had worked.'

'Knowing I didn't have much time before anybody else

found us, I quickly told them what to do. "Tell your friends about Dougal,' I instructed. "I want you *all* to come and watch the show we have created just for you. It will take place in the big barn next to my house. You know the one?" They both nodded, eyes slightly unfocused. "In two days then, after the noon bell sounds. Quickly, go!" They scampered off, a dreamy look on their faces. Biting my lip, I gathered up Dougal and the obstacle course and left.'

'I pulled the same trick at various locations throughout the town that day and the next. I knew I had to get *all* of the children excited about seeing the show, even the bigger ones. I just prayed the device would work on a crowd, or I would be doomed to kill those poor souls. I simply couldn't let that happen.'

'Some time before noon on the big day, I was nervously pacing the barn, hoping my plan would work. I had set up a huge course for Dougal this time, wanting to give the children at least one great show in their miserable lives, accompanied by my piping of course.'

'If any of the children showed up, that was. I heard the noon bell toll in the distance, but the path to the town remained deserted. After a while, my heart sank and I collapsed onto an old bale, wondering what to do next. I only had a few more days before the deadline, but couldn't think how else to get the children to safety in time. I decided I would move to another town rather than carry out the wicked request of the townsfolk.'

'Despondently, I walked over to the course, preparing to dismantle it. As I bent over, I heard the squeak of the old door hinge as it was cautiously pushed open. My heart raced and I turned to see dozens of grubby children stream into the barn, peering into the relative darkness. A wide smile split my face and I ushered them inside, telling them to sit and be comfortable.'

'Once the last straggler had tiptoed inside, I walked over to the course and introduced them to Dougal, who sat on my palm, quite unconcerned. I had made him a little hat that sat jauntily atop his little head, his ears poking through the slots. The wonder and amazement in their eyes as I made him jump, spin, and run up and down my arms warmed my heart. But the laughter when Dougal ran over my face and sat on my head, twitching his whiskers at his adoring crowd lifted my soul.'

'I think there were well over one hundred children in the barn that day. So many orphans with only themselves to watch out for each other. I was determined to help them have a better life.'

'I played a few sharp notes on my pipe, causing many to jump in surprise. "Now for the main show," I declared grandly, gesturing to the course behind me. "Who wants to place to cheese in the trap?" A host of small, grimy hands waved excitedly in the air.'

'I chose the smallest child there, a little girl shyly sucking her thumb. She smiled sweetly and hesitantly walked over towards me. "Say hello to Dougal, little one," I said gently, holding out my faithful rat. She sighed as she stroked his silky head, and giggled to hear him chatter contentedly. I passed her the cheese and told her where to put it.'

'"Now watch the amazing feats of Dougal the Rat as he navigates this amazing maze in search of treasure." I let go of the wriggling rodent and watched him race off as I played a merry tune. The children leaned closer to get a better look.'

'I didn't have the heart to use the device on them right then. They were having such a grand time, I doubt they had ever been entertained quite so much. As Dougal scampered up the last platform and began to gnaw at the cheese, I ended the music with a flourish. To tumultuous applause and loud cheers, I bowed several times with Dougal on my palm, his front paws waving in the air. "And now for our next trick," I shouted over the din of the crowd. They quieted quickly and looked at my expectantly.'

'I walked over to the barn door and dropped the heavy beam into place, locking us in. Slowly, I pulled the device out of my pocket. "'Ere, what's going on?" asked one of the older boys, immediately suspicious. "What's that thing in your hands?" The others picked up on his wary tone and began to climb to their feet, survival instincts kicking in. "Don't worry, I would never harm you," I reassured them, becoming somewhat alarmed as they grew dangerously silent and began to approach, some slipping knives out of hidden pockets. My hand shook, and Dougal disappeared beneath my jerkin, sensing the sudden tension.'

'As the mob drew closer, knocking over Dougal's course, I knew I had to act fast or be overwhelmed. Praying fervently that it would work on so many children at once, I triggered the device. Immediately their faces relaxed and they stopped, looking at me expectantly. I breathed a sigh of relief and wiped my brow.'

'"I will take you somewhere safe, away from the townsfolk who only want to hurt you. Father Conall will look after you, I'm sure." I hadn't actually asked him, you understand. But he was a kind man and head of a monastic school. I was sure he would be delighted to tame these lost souls and lead them to God.'

'"Follow me, young ones!" I ordered, lifting the bar and swinging wide the massive doors. Turning my back on the children, not without some trepidation, I strode into the warm afternoon sunshine. Luckily, they tagged along behind, a slightly absent look on every face. I was hoping *that* could be reversed once we reached safety.'

'I knew we had quite a hike ahead of us, so I decided to play cheerful song to lift our spirits. I must have looked quite a sight, playing my pipe while my bright rat catcher's coat streamed out behind me, leading the way for the throng of children. I could see the guards' heads bobbing along the wall as they tracked our progress, no doubt watching in amazement and fear. I guessed tongues would wag before long, and the whole town would know what I alone had managed to do. My heart swelled with pride and I gave them a salute as we skipped by on our way to the children's new future.'

'And that is how I managed to rid Hamelin of its pesky problem without harming a soul. Father Conall was indeed delighted to take the children under his wing. Especially when I assured him that Hamelin would contribute to their upkeep. Well, I couldn't let such a wonderful device go to waste, could I? The town leaders readily agreed to my demands after I had a few private words with them…'

'Yes, you're right. I realised quite quickly that it was hard to give up that infernal device. The temptation of being able to control those who had previously mocked me almost proved to be my undoing. Only through sheer will did I manage to resist. Walking to an old abandoned well that I had discovered in the gentle hills surrounding the town, I threw it into the dark depths. I only felt a few pangs of regret as it tumbled through the air. I didn't hear it splash as it reached the bottom, so assumed it would be deep enough that no-one else would ever find it again.'

'As for the townsfolk, they never did thank me for what I had done. But I don't mind too much. They are wary of me now, half believing that I have special powers, and afford me a little more respect. Although not too much, as I had also commanded them to build an orphanage and school for any stragglers that remained. Their lighter wallets didn't help to endear me. But it's much better to look after our lost ones than to abandon them to cruel fate, I say.'

'How *did* you hear about me anyway? The townsfolk really don't like to talk about that little episode in our lives. I think they're ashamed, to be honest. As they should be!'

'What do you mean, I'm in a well-known fairy tale? Please don't be ridiculous. Tell me the truth or I will bid you good day.'

'Are seriously trying to tell me that you're from the future, and that a "Mr B" helped you travel through a hole in the sky like the one I saw? Well really, I don't quite know what to say. Your story is rather unbelievable, what kind of fool do you take me for?'

'Now, if you don't mind I have rats to catch and I refuse to spend another moment listening to a mad woman. It's clear you've got a tale of your own to tell, but I don't want to hear it and become infected by your insanity, thank you very much. Maybe you should talk to Father Conall, he is much better at helping poor, damaged souls like yourself.'

'Go on, off you go. And mind you don't knock that trap on your way out. Herr Schmidt will be extremely annoyed if I don't catch these rats, and I need the money. I don't have time for your absurd ideas. Fairy tales indeed, what utter nonsense…'

THE SIMPLE TRUTH

'That's the last one. Finally, I can rest. Tracking down those so-called villains has been hard work, I'm exhausted.'

'I *am* hoping these accounts will put the record straight though. Those fairy tales are just that – stories based on a grain or two of truth. Clearly, reality was much stranger.'

'I suppose I should tell you my own story, so you know why I began this quest. Let me see, where to begin? I've been back and forwards through time so often, I hardly know *when* I am.'

'I guess my life changed forever not long before I met Snow White...'

'That wasn't her real name, of course. She was born Neve, but I playfully called her Snow White because her face was so pale against her dark raven hair. Those luscious red lips really did look like drops of blood on icy snow. And she wasn't a little girl, far from it. Although I admit she *was* a little younger than me. No, she was my one true love and our souls were entwined. We used to tease each other, as sweethearts like to do. "Who is the fairest of them all?" "I am!" "No…I am," and so on, until we laughingly covered each other with tender kisses.'

'I wasn't an evil Queen either. I am not even human, if you must know. But close enough that my Neve never realised. My mother called me Ceridwen, which means *blessed* on my world. I grew up as she did, trained in a scientific discipline from an early age. We were a sophisticated race, celebrated for our knowledge throughout the advanced worlds.'

'I qualified as a chemical engineer, but discovered early on that my true talents lay in mixing substances for healing. So I learned to recognise most ailments and how to treat them with whatever materials were available on a planet. Some of the more backwards societies called it sorcery. But my abilities are simply the result of many years of hard work acquiring knowledge, skills and experience across the galaxies.'

'It was when I was involved in a particularly challenging case that I somehow ended up on this…dirtball. I'm sorry to be so dismissive, but this world really hasn't developed properly, based on what I've observed so far. And you poor people are doomed, if Alice is to be believed. There may be salvation if attitudes change, but I'm not hopeful.'

'I was walking through the woods collecting certain herbs that I knew would make an effective healing potion, when a large hole appeared right in front of me. I barely had time to scream before it sucked me through and spat me face first into a prickly bush. Stunned, I scrambled free from the sharp leaves hooking my skin, and lay on my back to catch my breath. The sight of the single yellow sun glaring down at me shocked me to the core, as only moments ago two dull red suns had hung in the sky.'

'I realised immediately, of course, that I must have travelled through a wormhole. After all, that *was* how we were able to travel the galaxies. But it was clearly an uncontrolled one, not the established ones that we have learned to use. The idea that it was actually a timehole didn't even cross my mind at that point. All such thoughts were swept away when Neve stumbled across me.'

'Literally, as it happens. She tripped over my legs as I lay sprawled across the path and fell into my arms, banging her head against mine. It may simply have been concussion, but I saw stars when I first glimpsed those big eyes looking down at me in concern. My fate was settled in that moment.'

'She had herself been looking for something that might help heal her father, who was deathly ill. After we had talked for a while, her soft hands clasped in mine as we sat on the stony path, she discovered that I was a healer and immediately dragged me to my feet. "You must help him, Ceri, please. I will be bereft without him." Nodding, I gestured for her to lead the way and followed, unable to stop myself admiring her smooth, lithe legs as she ran ahead.'

'I saw at once that the frail man wouldn't be much longer for this world. His yellowing eyes and the tenderness above his liver told me all I needed to know. Sadly, he died a few days after I arrived, despite my best efforts. Neve was inconsolable and spent many hours in my arms while she wept. I vowed then that my life would be devoted to protecting her from further harm. It breaks my heart to admit that I have failed so dismally.'

'After her father's burial, our friendship began to grow. We declared our love for each other one glorious evening under the stars. I was the happiest woman alive, despite the knowledge that I had landed in a truly primitive society. An ingrained belief in black magic was widespread, and witch trials were a regular occurrence. I quickly became a target, mistrusted despite my many successes at healing folk from miles around. The death of Neve's much-loved father never left the minds of the superstitious locals, who believed that I had dabbled in the dark arts so I could have my wicked way with their precious Neve. Still, we managed to live our lives in relative peace…until those wretched Tamarians destroyed it all.'

'The villagers called the small, strange creatures dwarfs, and almost revered them. They would fling open their windows and watch in fascination as the little men marched past with their beards wrapped round their waists, chanting as they tramped to the mine. While six of the dwarfs worked deep in the bowels of the earth, a watchman would remain outside, brandishing his pickaxe at anyone who dared to venture near. A surly bunch, of that there was no doubt. At the end of each day, they would triumphantly bring out a nugget of gold to sell to the highest bidder.'

'But from the start, I had my suspicions. After all, I *did* have a lot of experience with alien lifeforms. To my mind, they very much resembled the Tamarians, a space-faring, very long-lived race that regularly formed fearsome clans and roamed the stars to steal from others. And who were well-known for inventing the transmogrifier, a device capable of giving any object the illusion of gold. My hunch was confirmed when I happened to overhear them talking.'

'Wait…I should be truthful with myself, at least. I was eavesdropping. I wanted to find out who they really were, so I sneaked over to their little cottage in the woods and crept around until I found an open window. I have a curious nature, I can't help nosing around. And to be brutally honest, despite my love for Neve I was lonely for someone who would understand where I came from, who might even have visited my home world. I longed to reminisce about the majestic mountains shrouded in perpetual mist, and the two moons that would peek over the horizon as darkness fell. I was homesick, pure and simple. I think part of me hoped that if they *were* Tamarians, they would still have their spaceship and I could take my beloved Neve home to meet my family.'

'It seems I had caught them in the middle of a heated argument. Once they'd finished yelling, savagely pulling beards and poking rotund bellies, they settled down around the large wooden table, onto which the largest, meanest-looking dwarf loudly thumped his fist before beginning his tirade. "Now that we've *finally* found the ore, what are we going to do with it? We've spent years digging away in that blasted rock, yet only now do you tell me that we don't have the first clue how to convert it to fuel. Boneheads, the whole lot of you. We're stuck on this primitive planet, surrounded by ignorant fools who barely have enough knowledge to create fire, let alone fuel a spaceship. We're never going to get back to Tamaris at this rate." He sighed, tiredly rubbing his grubby face before glaring at the others. "Well, any bright ideas?" My heart raced as I listened to his deep, gravelly voice, knowing there might be a chance to return home after all.'

'I was a chemical engineer, remember. I knew I had the skills to convert the ore, even with the few simple tools available in this world. So I stupidly decided to intervene. "I can help you," I called through the open window, stepping back in alarm when the dwarfs immediately rushed over, pickaxes raised. "Get her, lads!" roared the leader, pushing open the glass and climbing through. I held up my hands in supplication and waited for him to approach, flinching as he laid the sharp point of his axe against my throat. "Why are you spying on us, lassie?" he asked, his voice dangerously low. The other Tamarians circled round, glowering and itching to use their weapons.'

'Swallowing nervously, I quickly explained. "I'm not from this planet either, I am from Wissen. My speciality means I can be very useful to you." I watched in satisfaction at the surprise and delight that lit their faces. As I said, my people are widely known, and it was clear the Tamarians immediately recognised my worth. I breathed a sigh of relief as the axe was slowly lowered. "I think you'd better come in and have a brew, my lady. We have a lot to talk about." I rubbed my throat, looking warily at the small muscular men still surrounding me, then shrugged and followed him inside.'

'We spent the rest of the day looking at the ore and discussing what apparatus would be needed to smelt and extract the rare metal, then combine it with the right chemicals to make fuel. It would be a lengthy, complicated process and I warned them repeatedly that it would take a long time before we had enough fuel not only to take off, but to reach civilisation once more. They also let me see their ship, concealed deep within a well-hidden cave. The sight of it strengthened my resolve to help, despite my natural distrust of them. Everyone knew that Tamarians were quick to betray business partners, and only the truly desperate would make a deal with them.'

'I decided to set up the manufacturing process in the house I shared with Neve. It had belonged to her landowner father, a large, sprawling building surrounded by several outhouses. I planned to use one of those, if I could find the right equipment. I certainly kept the blacksmith busy during the first month or two, creating all sorts of instruments that I knew I would need. By the end, I could tell he was wary of what strange item I would ask for next. I also managed to find a glassblower to make some bottles and flasks and the pipes to connect them all. It was a lengthy process and by the time I was ready to go, the dwarfs were already restless.'

'The smoke that billowed out from the roof as I smelted the ore, combined with the colourful gases and noxious odours that escaped when I converted it to fuel, cemented the locals' view that I was an evil witch. Luckily, they had too much love for Neve to approach me directly, and too much fear of me. As for Neve, she supported my work, especially when I explained I was helping the dwarfs. She loved the little men, regularly cleaning their cottage and cooking for them even before I arrived. She was that kind of woman – hard-working, kind, always willing to help those who lived on her land. My heart swelled every time I saw her bake a pudding to cheer up a sick child or stretch her aching back after digging over the garden for one of the old ones. She was a treasure, my Neve.'

'It was several months later when the dwarfs acted. They had been growing increasingly impatient, despite my reassurances that the lengthy time was normal and that I had already started to produce some fuel. But they were a suspicious bunch who would double-cross anybody – naturally, they assumed I would do the same to them. They thought I had been siphoning off fuel and was planning to steal their ship. A ridiculous notion, and I told them as much using language that would have made a sailor blush. I was hot, grimy, tired

A Likely Story

of spending day after day in that sweltering room, and in no mood for accusations.'

'As my voice got louder and more shrill, I could see the dwarfs looking at each other under their lashes. I should have realised then that something was up, when Arzt gently patted me on the arm and soothingly told me not to worry. He said they knew I would do *exactly* as they asked. But I was too angry and upset to take much notice of the smirks that passed between them. He gave me a quick, surprising hug and an irritating pat on the bottom, then led his dwarfs out. Frowning, I carried on with my work.'

'I worked long into the night to finish the latest stage of fuel synthesis, finally stumbling out of the stuffy room into the cool, moonlit garden, breathing deeply of the crisp air. Vigorously rubbing my dry eyes, I slowly walked across the dewy grass to the house, stretching out the kinks along the way. I was very much looking forward to a hug from Neve and some much-needed sleep.'

'It took me a long moment to realise that the Neve-shaped mound under the covers was in fact several plump cushions. Confused, fatigue dulling my senses, I padded to the other bedrooms, wondering if she had fallen asleep there instead. There was no response to my frantic calling as I threw aside the bed covers. Panic-stricken and now wide awake, I rushed downstairs and searched every room, then all of the outhouses. It wasn't until I slumped on a dining chair, exhausted and worried, that I spotted the parchment on the table. My eyes widened in horror as I read the words.'

"'We don't like betrayal. Neve is ours until you've finished the fuel. She won't be harmed...unless my boys get impatient. So hurry." The cheap parchment crumpled as I clenched my fist, furious.'

'After some time, I managed to calm myself and think more clearly. I had to find Neve and make her safe. At first light, I would swallow my anger and visit the Tamarians, try to negotiate her freedom. But I didn't hold out much hope, they were a stubborn race. I could simply refuse to make more fuel, but knew I would never see her again if so. If they wouldn't release her, or even let me speak to her, I would have to take more drastic measures. At the very least, I needed to find out where they were keeping her captive so I could arrange a rescue.'

'The meeting went pretty much as I expected. They laughed when I asked to see her, telling me she was safe in their stasis chamber. My heart sank at the thought of that vibrant woman frozen within the narrow, transparent cubicle I had seen on the ship. Only the fingerprints and retinal scan of a Tamarian would unlock the vessel – I would have to capture one alone if I wanted to rescue Neve. To buy some time while I worked out a plan, I agreed to speed up the manufacturing process as best as I could, so long as they didn't harm Neve. Head bowed in apparent defeat, I slowly walked away, plotting my next move.'

'I disguised myself before returning to the cottage.

During my training, I had practiced several methods of temporarily ageing the skin, and I decided to pretend to be an old woman selling ribbons and apples. Those dwarfs loved the sweet crops that grew in our orchard, and Neve had often baked them apple pie. One of them would be tempted to taste the fruit, which would be drenched in a strong sleeping potion.'

'I spent the next few days roaming the forest, searching for the plants I would need. The locals clearly became concerned by my incoherent mumbling and dishevelled appearance, but none found the courage to approach me. Apart from one small child who bravely tugged my sleeve to ask, "Where's my Nevie gone?" I tried to hide my tears as I said she had gone to visit family for a while, and would be "back soon, I promise." Her beaming face made me even more determined to succeed.'

'After a long night spent boiling and distilling to extract the essence of the plants, I finally managed to combine them correctly to make two potions, one to age my face and the other to spread on the apples. The latter was intended to induce a deep sleep, but it was impossible to accurately gauge the strength of the drug; it was just as likely to kill one of the small creatures. But I was past caring, despite my vow as a healer not to cause harm.'

'I slept fitfully for a few hours, before getting up to display the ribbons and apples in a wicker basket. Removing the stopper from a glass flask, I liberally applied the sleeping potion to the apples, making them glisten invitingly. Hoping that I had remembered the correct formula, I apprehensively began to apply the ageing lotion to my face, neck and arms. Watching the skin tighten and wrinkle was a most unpleasant experience, especially when I caught my reflection in the looking glass. *Not the fairest of them all now*, I thought to myself sadly, the withered face of a crone looking back at me. I sighed, wrapped an old shawl around my head, hunched my shoulders, and picked up the basket. Making sure nobody was around, I set off down the path towards the dwarfs' cottage.'

'It took me longer than normal to reach it, hampered as I was by my disguise and trudging along like an old woman. I practiced a few cackles along the way, partly to amuse myself but mostly to settle my nerves. The stakes were high, and I didn't want to make any mistakes. I tried to calm my rapid heartbeat and breathlessness when I saw Artz loitering outside the house, smoking a pungent pipe. I coughed to get his attention, then limped slowly towards him.

"Hello young man," I wheezed, peering down into his face. "Would you like to buy one of my beautiful apples? Freshly picked this morning." He looked at me dismissively, reaching out to pluck one from the basket. "Why don't I try it for free," he said, sneering at me. "If I like it, I won't kick your scrawny backside for trespassing." I glared at him resentfully, but pretended I was cowed. I didn't want his money, only his fingertips and eyes.'

'As we stood there, low voices drifted through the kitchen window. Trying not to look too interested, I listened intently as Artz mockingly tossed the apple from one hand to the other, teasing me. "It was bloody heavy that stasis chamber, I can tell you. We were sweating by the time we'd taken it out of the ship and hidden it, weren't we Blöd?" I heard a mumble of assent. "Took us ages to set up the solar panel, as well, bleeding insects crawling all over the place. It's a wonder anything works in this godforsaken place. At least no-one will find her, we managed to get the cloaking device working right enough, didn't we Blöd?" Another quiet murmur agreed.'

'My heart sank when I realised my plan would no longer work. Neve wasn't even on the ship and would be impossible to find unless somebody happened to stumble over her. But the Tamarians weren't likely to use a well-trodden path as a hiding place. I had to find out where she was first, before I could do anything.

'During my momentary distraction, Artz had opened his mouth to take a huge bite of the apple. "No, dear sir!" I cried, snatching it from his hand. "These apples aren't good enough for you, I just saw a fat worm poking his head through the skin. Forgive me, I shall bring you a new basket for free." With that, I quickly scurried away, turning my head only once to see Artz staring at me suspiciously. He stroked his beard and frowned, watching as I almost ran away.'

'Later that afternoon, once I had recovered my composure, I buried the apples deep in the midden heap. Wanting to clear my head, I went for a short walk, hoping for inspiration. The ageing potion had already worn off, and I was relieved to see the wrinkles disappear as my skin regained its elasticity.'

'I still had no idea how to rescue Neve by the time I returned. As I strolled along, lost in thought, I glimpsed a small figure skulking around the back of the house. Quickly, I hid so I could watch more closely. My eyes widened to see Artz emerge with the basket and ribbons, realisation dawning on his face. His anger as he stalked back down the path through the forest left me in dread of his likely retaliation. Had I already put Neve's life further in danger?'

The next day he paid me a visit, sauntering into my kitchen with a dangerous grin on his face. "So you thought you could fool me, did you? I expect that apple was poisoned?" His face darkened as I raised an eyebrow. His jaw clenched and it was a moment before he could continue.'

'Glaring at me, he took something out of his pocket and began turning it over and over in his large palms. "We found this at the bottom of an old, abandoned well, dearie. Maybe you have an idea what it does, seeing as you're so well educated and all that?" He held out his hand to display a small, metallic object. Curiosity aroused, I reached out to touch it but he quickly snatched it away.'

'"We only discovered its powers when I accidently triggered the device during one of my daily arguments with that idiot Blöd. He spent the rest of the day trying to kick his own backside. Saved me the trouble, I'm happy to say." My mouth gaped as his words. Surely no society had been stupid enough to actually *make* a mind control device. And how had such a sophisticated weapon ended up on this backwards world anyway?'

'"What do I care about such things?" I said, nonchalantly. "All Wissen are trained to resist mind control from a very early age. We developed the technology to create such a weapon centuries ago, but discarded it because of the potential for great harm. It will not work against me." I gave him a withering look. "Go on, try it." He scowled ferociously as he aimed at me and pressed the trigger.'

'It was powerful, I can attest to that. Despite many years spent learning to create strong mental barriers, I could feel my mind becoming fuzzy around the edges. Closing my eyes, I concentrated hard so I could fully barricade myself against the onslaught. Once I was sure of my defences, I looked at Artz and smirked.'

'"Damn you woman!" he cried, when he realised I could not be controlled. "You will regret crossing me. I promise you will spend the rest of your days wondering when we'll be coming for you. We *will* have our revenge, and our fuel. And Neve will never be yours again." He hawked, spat on the floor, then stormed out, slamming the door behind him.'

'I stood there trembling for some time, both in fear and anger. Not only was Neve even further from safety, I had the added problem of the mind control device. It simply couldn't remain in the hands of the ruthless Tamarians, I would have to retrieve it from them. And now, more than anything, I wanted to go home, the longing almost overwhelming me.'

'I decided I would finish making the fuel, as it was my only hope of leaving this place. I spent an anxious couple of weeks worrying about Neve, constantly looking over my shoulder and expecting Artz to appear with his sharp axe. Yet despite his threats, I heard nothing further. By the time I had finished the fuel and hidden it in an old, abandoned hut, I was hoping he had calmed down enough for me to negotiate a deal. Safe passage for me and Neve in return for the fuel. I began to make my way to his cottage.'

'Wearily, I plodded along, wishing I'd could have been satisfied with my life instead of scheming with those treacherous Tamarians. Life had been simpler and much sweeter before I started yearning for a foolish fantasy. As I walked, I wondered whether I would even be able tell Neve the whole truth. It would shake her whole foundation, topple every belief she held. Reality might destroy her innocent nature, and I wasn't sure I could do that to her.'

'Preoccupied, I failed to hear the clamouring of a small crowd that had gathered on the village green. It was the sound of Artz demanding attention that alerted me to possible danger. Keeping close to a wall, I sidled around a house and took cover behind a wagon to get a better look.

"'She is a witch!" he cried, brandishing his pickaxe in

the air. "She communicates with the devil to perform her magic. You've all seen the fumes of hell pouring from her house late at night." He swept his gaze around the crowd. "And now your cherished Neve has disappeared. Do you truly doubt that Ceridwen was responsible?"'

'I was heartened to see uncertainty on many faces. "Neve loved her, we know that much," shouted Elisabeth, the matronly baker. She turned her large, red face to the crowd. "We might have strong concerns about Ceri's nightly activities. But surely we must trust Neve, and believe that she would never harm her?" The crowd rumbled in agreement.'

'Realising he was starting to lose their attention, Artz raised his voice once more. "Ceri is a beautiful woman...and she is incredibly vain. You all know the lengths she went to obtain a looking glass." I cursed my simple desire for normality, which had led me to search far and wide for someone who could make me a decent mirror. "She couldn't bear the fact that Neve's beauty surpassed her own, and wanted her dead. Neve hasn't gone to visit her family – she was poisoned by that vile woman."'

'As he spoke, he hung his head and gestured to a covered wagon. Blöd rolled aside the heavy tarpaulin and the crowd gasped in horror to see the glass 'coffin' and beautiful Neve lying inside, unbreathing. The sight of her pale face surrounded by that halo of dark hair wrenched my heart and I stood up. "No!" I cried, tears trickling down my face. "I would never hurt her, she is still alive. These dwarfs are trying to trick you, to make me do their bidding. You must believe me." I looked imploringly at the crowd, then stepped back in alarm at their fury. "You killed her, you witch," shouted Elisabeth, grief twisting her face. "How can you claim that she is alive? Look at her, as still as death. Do you take us for simple fools?" She used her bulk to force her way through the crowd to the communal cookfire. Grabbing a burning branch, she lifted it high in the air. "You are a killer, an evil witch, and you will pay. Get her," she screamed, and the crowd surged forward.'

'As I turned to run, I heard Artz cackle in glee. "Don't kill her just yet," he yelled, his voice cutting through the angry shouts of the mob. "We want her to suffer for a long time." I quickened my pace, terror galvanising me. I had no friends to protect me, no safe haven in which to hide. I was like a hunted fox who would be ripped to shreds by the bloodlust of the hounds. I fled blindly into the forest, hoping to lose their scent.'

'It seemed that I ran for a long time, pursued by the enraged villagers, the dwarfs capering along excitedly. I wondered at their stamina, as many of the people chasing me were old and must surely be running out of energy. I risked a glance behind and was shocked to see them struggling for breath, faces an alarming red, chests heaving in exertion. I put on a burst of speed that surely none could match, only to hear their pace increase. I turned back once more to see Artz grinning madly, waving the mind control device over his head.'

A Likely Story

'I realised then he must have used it, that the villagers would never stop chasing me until they dropped dead. I had to find a solution before I inadvertently killed them all. I swerved off the path and plunged into the undergrowth, heading towards the old hut. My last desperate hope was to threaten to blow up the fuel unless Artz let me and Neve go.'

'I scrambled through the thickets, my hair getting caught on sharp twigs and brambles scraping my skin. I could hear thrashing behind me as the tired men and women followed as best they could, unable to give up. My heart sank to see the smaller dwarfs moving through the dense growth with relative ease. They were almost upon me as I half fell into the small clearing. I stood for a moment in front of the dilapidated hut, trying to catch my breath, then hurriedly turned back to face Artz.'

'"Don't come any closer," I warned, taking something out of my pocket and holding it high. "I have primed the fuel and it *will* explode if I press this button. It will kill us all, but you have taken everything from me so I no longer care." Artz lifted his hand to stop anybody from approaching. "Come on now Ceri, don't do anything daft. We were only having a bit of fun, weren't we lads?" The other dwarfs nodded, glancing at each other uncertainly. The villagers slumped to the floor, panting and utterly exhausted. "You can have Neve back in exchange for the fuel, how about that? We only want to get off this rotten planet, we don't care about you. Do we have a deal?" I watched his face as I rubbed my thumb over the tinderbox in my hand. He must know that I was bluffing, but I guess he had to make sure. I sighed, then nodded in submission.'

'As I cautiously stepped backwards to the locked door of the hut, a fierce glow bathed the scrubby glade, illuminating the stunned faces gaping at something behind me. Confused, I turned around – and fell straight into another of those damned wormholes. My last sight as I twisted and tumbled was of Artz leaping towards me and tripping, the mind control device slipping from his hands and hitting me squarely on the forehead before the hole shut down. Darkness fell and I knew no more.'

'And that's how I ended up in this time. I didn't realise at first, of course, when I blearily woke face down in a kitchen garden, nose mashed into a large cabbage. The sound of heavy footsteps thundering down the stone path energised me. I scrambled to my feet as a truly enormous woman lumbered towards me, a metal spade swinging effortlessly above her head. "Get out of there, you little thief!" she roared, her voice resonating deep within my chest.'

'As I ran, stumbling over lines of carrots and ducking between strings of beans, my eyes widened to see a car in the driveway and a warm glow from an electric lamp lighting a downstairs window. I knew then that I was no longer in Neve's world. Grief-stricken, I was overwhelmed by dark despair.'

'It took me a long time to recover myself. I wandered the streets, begging for food and stealing clothes so I wouldn't attract too much attention. I had nowhere to go, no-one to help me, and no hope of ever seeing Neve again. I truly didn't know what to do next, despite all my learning.'

'Then one bleak day I passed a library. It was cold and wet, and I was shivering and so tired. I decided to go inside to warm up at least. As I walked through the doors, warm air redolent with the scent of paper books washed over me. I sniffed deeply, the smell taking me back to happier times. When I looked more closely, I saw it must be a place for children, with brightly coloured pictures on the walls and little faces peering excitedly between the pages of their books. I smiled, my hurt easing a little, then looked down to see a small child plucking at my dirty coat. "Read me a story," she begged, pulling me over to a small table and chair. "My favourite one," she added, pushing a large book into my hands. I raised my eyebrows at her, then turned to look at the cover. My heart almost stopped to see a drawing of my Neve in her glass coffin. "What the…," I whispered, tracing my fingers over the painted face. Eyes wide, I opened the book and began to read.'

'And *that* is how I first read the story of Snow White and the Seven Dwarfs. The little girl wandered away as I sat absorbed, reading the twisted lies that had been written about me. I was stunned by the realisation that the fairy tale was set in the past, implying I had somehow travelled through time. Thoughts whirling, I read all of the tales in the book, then sat back in amazement and cold fury. Suddenly, I pushed back the chair and stalked into the fresh air, the storybook still in my hands. I wanted answers so I could find my way back to Neve. Maybe the people who lived in the house where I landed could help me. It was a starting place, at least. Although I hoped to avoid another encounter with that gargantuan woman – I *did* still value my life. I cleaned myself up, stole a new outfit, then went to investigate further.'

'A little research back in the library led me to Mr Blunderbore and reports of his experiments in quantum physics. Hope flaring, I paid him a visit. As you have already heard, he wasn't creating standard wormholes but timeholes. As I listened to him talk, I was amazed to note certain similarities between his story and that of *Jack and the Beanstalk*, described in the book I kept close at hand. I had already met his wife in the garden, and could well believe that Jack had exaggerated her into a giant who lived in a huge house surrounded by massive devices. The theory was no more fantastical than my own tale, although I am not sure I convinced Mr B.'

'After I left his house, rather hurriedly when I heard his wife approaching, I wandered the streets for a while, trying to plan my next steps. I knew I would have to go back and demand help from Mr B. An appeal to his insatiable curiosity should prove irresistible. My thoughts scattered when a bus rumbled through a large puddle, drenching me in cold, muddy water.'

'As I stood there, dripping and cursing the driver, an

advert emblazoned across the side of the bus caught my eye. It wasn't so much the title that grabbed my attention, although I was somewhat intrigued as to whether *Snow and the Dwarfs, the True Story* could live up to its name. No, it was the sight of one of the dwarfs grinning down at me. If he wasn't a Tamarian, I had wasted my many years of training. I knew I would have to speak to the actor.'

'I was very much surprised to hear Lorcan's story of *Rumpelstiltskin*, another well-known fairy tale and yet another link to Mr Blunderbore. I guessed it was *his* transmogrifier that had ended up in Mr B's hands. The Dranghesi who had been trying to capture Lorcan must have been trapped on Earth by Mr B's timehole. It made me even more determined to pay him another visit.'

'He was "most flabbergasted and appalled" when I told him my story, and truly apologetic at disrupting my life so thoroughly. But he was tremendously excited to realise his timeholes had managed to pierce time *and* space. "No wonder my equations weren't correct!" he exclaimed. His first trial had brought me to Earth in the past, while his tinkering with those calculations catapulted me centuries into the future and to his door.'

'I begged him to send me back to Neve. But although he had almost perfected the technique of opening and closing the timeholes safely, he said it would take a long time to unravel the complex calculations involved in reopening my own timehole, given the extra dimension of also travelling across space. I had to be patient until he could safely send me back in time – unless I would rather return to my home planet? Part of me was tempted, I will admit. But Neve was still trapped, her radiant soul suspended in stasis. I had to release her. Besides, I wanted revenge on those seven dwarfs. They had kidnapped Snow and made out that *I* was the villain.'

'I met with Mr B often after that. While I waited impatiently for him to solve my problem, I decided to see whether my hypothesis was correct – were Blunderbore's timeholes responsible for any more of the fairy tales in my book? I asked if he could determine when and where each of his rather unstable timeholes had opened. I wanted to dig around a little, see if any of the tales could be related to actual events reported around those times.'

'I decided to begin with Mr B's own tale, doing some research at Jack's end of the timehole. Eventually, I stumbled across a few newspaper reports of Jack 'The Bard' Durden, a wealthy merchant who claimed his fortune was made by some golden eggs. He insisted they had been stolen by the notorious thieves Wolfie and Red, and I found several rather lurid reports about both criminals. I longed to speak to them, and asked Mr B whether it would be safe to reopen their timehole. He reluctantly agreed, as long as I promised I would only talk, sternly warning me not to do anything that would affect the timeline. Seeing the look on my face, it seems he altered his calculations so that I arrived sometime after the key events. After hearing Wolfie's version of *Little*

Red Riding Hood, I realised he was another person who had been wrongly vilified, a kindred spirit.'

'In the meantime, Mr Blunderbore had discovered that not only had his very first experiment brought me from Wissen to Earth, but had also trapped somebody from the far future. Further research on my part led me to Mary, now working in the café. I had set up a search for any newspaper reports on 'time travel', which had flagged up the unusual case of a woman held in a psychiatric hospital some years ago for her unwavering belief that she had travelled through time. I made Mr B hack into the hospital computers to gain access to her files, and discovered her insistence that her story was the basis of *Alice in Wonderland*. I went to visit her, only a short ride away on the bus, and my suspicions were confirmed.'

'When I related her story to Mr B, he realised that the timehole must have split as Alice didn't arrive in the present time with Mary. Scrutinising his calculations unearthed the deviation, and I was able to dredge up the historic and now public records of an old asylum in Germany, which not only detailed the prominent case of Alice, but also revealed the dishonest transactions by Doctor Gothel. As before, Mr B wouldn't let me interfere with events so I talked to the Doctor afterwards and discovered the true tale of *Rapunzel*.'

'I was still confused how the seven Tamarians in my time had managed to get hold of the mind control device that Alice had used to torment Mary's villagers. I asked Mr B whether this particular timehole could actually have split three ways, as there were no records of it arriving with Alice at the asylum. He was elated at the prospect, and spent many hours poring over his equations once more.'

'When he found the third thread, my heart raced to hear that it had opened in Hamelin, only a few years before my own time with Neve. Everybody knew the tale of the *Pied Piper*, so Mr B didn't seem overly suspicious when I said I wanted to investigate. I tried to contain my excitement at finally getting back to Neve's time. I knew I would be able to change what had happened to us both by not agreeing to make fuel for those blasted Tamarians in the first place.'

'But he was shrewder than I thought, and his mind was unclouded by love and revenge. He knew when Neve had been captured and realised, of course, that I would naturally want to change time and avoid all of my pain. Taking me gently by the hand, he sat me down and explained why that would be impossible. The version of me in the past would still be there – which meant that if I somehow managed to stop myself from making the fuel, I wouldn't then travel to the future, and therefore wouldn't be able to come back to persuade me not to make the fuel…a paradox that couldn't be allowed to happen. I could only travel to a point after the timehole had reopened, and hope to rescue Snow from then onwards. I was furious and heartsick, unwilling to accept the truth. But eventually my scientific training kicked in, and I reluctantly acknowledged that he was right.'

'After visiting Hamelin, the problem of the mind control device still bothered me. Aldred told me he had thrown it down an abandoned well, which explained how my Tamarians had discovered it. But when Artz accidentally flung it into the timehole that swallowed me, it hadn't landed alongside me in Mrs Blunderbore's vegetable patch. I suspected that my own timehole might also have split. Mr B was sorely perplexed when he finally discovered that the device – first used by Alice on poor Mary, then by Aldred on the children, and finally by the seven dwarfs on the villagers – had actually ended up in the future. The other end of the hole appeared in Alice's own time in the future, near the institute in which she was later held captive. I can only assume that the owners found it and realised its potential, then tested it out on the children. Another paradox, which kept Mr B occupied for hours – how was the device ever made in the first place?'

'Mr Blunderbore has a lot to answer for, that much is clear. The truth was, he was meddling in things he didn't fully understand, causing chaos to people from all times and places. I was amazed to see how many of these people's stories had ended up as much-loved fairy tales – none of which would have existed if he had kept his curiosity to safer pastimes. I wonder how many more can be traced back to his interference. One thing is clear, however – the truth is not always what it seems. We should never blindly accept anything as fact without first doing our own research.'

'Mr B tells me he has almost unravelled my way back to Neve, so I am preparing to finally rescue her – her happy ending belongs with me, not Prince Charming. Maybe I'll go and see Wolfie first, take him up on his offer. He clearly wasn't happy where he was and we'd be stronger together, a great team to defeat those Tamarians. I think I've discovered a taste for adventure, if truth be told.'

'I must go, I'm sorry. My tale here is done and I have lots to plan and do. My Snow is waiting…'

FUMBLING SOUNDS. RECORDING ENDS

A NOTE FROM THE AUTHOR

Normally I write about medical problems and how to treat them. So I've had real fun telling you the true stories behind these much-loved fairy tales. I hope you enjoyed them!

If so, you might also like to hear Evie's tale – a girl who discovers she can travel the quantum net that connects us all, and who is pursued by the power-hungry Agathe. Read her story in 'Connected', the first book in the Naquant Traveller series, available now on Amazon.

If you liked my books, it would make me very happy if you could leave a review on Amazon. Such reviews are essential for any self-published author, so I would appreciate your help.

Printed in Great Britain
by Amazon